The Square Root of Truth

Joe McClain Jr.

Contents

DEDICATION

This book is dedicated to the memory of my late father Joe "Tana" McClain Sr. I hope that I can live up to legacy you left behind. In addition, this book is also dedicated to the memory of the father of my brother, Darius Johnson, Mr. Donald Butler.

ACKNOWLEDGMENTS

I don't even know where to begin with this book. 2018 has by far been the most turbulent year of my life. Let's start things off form the top. My wife, she had not one, not two, but three brain procedures. That was a roller coaster event in itself. In the midst of all that, things still didn't work out. I went through a divorce, something that no one ever wants to deal with. I have nothing negative to say on her and wish her all the best. Immediately after that it seemed, my beautiful Godmother suffered a cardiac episode and will never be the same again. Then, I thought it couldn't get any worse.

However, on May 21st, my father passed away. What made it worse is that I was out to sea at this moment. Now, let that sink in. Brain surgery, a divorce, Godmother's heart attack and then the death of your father. That's enough to drive anyone up the wall. Add in a move to another duty station for the military, and you can say that my life took on a mind of its own. For most people, this would be enough to put a bullet in your head. At times, I didn't think things could get any worse, but it did. I also struggled with a very bad addiction, that I am so desperately trying to get over. It's difficult, but I am trying. No, it's not drugs or anything harming my body, but like most people, I have my skeletons in the closet as well. So, in that regard, just say a quick prayer to whoever you pray to for your fellow author. On a brighter note, let me really take time to those who made this year amazing.

My man's Marcedes Lewis and his mom, Yvonne Snow-Withers. Yeah, I said that right. Marcedes Lewis, the 13-year tight end veteran of the Green Bay Packers and formerly the Jacksonville Jaguars. To allow me to be involved with the great work you two do for the community, I am humbled.

Thank you. Cyhi the Prince. My man's!!! I remember the day in San Diego where you performed with Krit. I waited for two hours just to see you. You didn't have to accept my book as a gift, but you did and rapped with me as if you knew me for a lifetime. I appreciate you much man. Troy Ave, you kept it real with me when you came out here. You weren't a big reader at all, but you still rocked with me and I'm humbled.

Big Duke, Darius Philon of the San Diego Chargers. Our text messages and phone calls are nothing but motivation. Keep grinding. I know that you have a long NFL career ahead of you.

Reggie Bush. Bruh!!! You always hold it down for San Diego and do great things through your charity weekend. I am honored to always attend and donate to great causes. Bruce Miller, former 49ers fullback, I remember our talk. I hope you start up everything within the S.T.E.M. program that you aspire. You are an inspiration.

And while I'm on the topic of the NFL. T.O. Mister Terrell Owens. Hall of Famer. A man, let me personally apologize for interrupting you while you were eating at Reggie's event. I sometimes lose focus and I didn't mean any disrespect brother. Just trying to bestow a gift on you. Again, apologies.

Kendall Gaskins, Lance Moore, Andre Reed, Tim Brown, much love to all of you gentleman. And to all who have supported myself and Uprock Publications, I thank you genuinely.

HOW WE GOT HERE

"BEFORE I HAND out my sentence, is there anything you would like to say to the court Mr. King?"

"Yes, your honor." A pause came over the courtroom as I looked around at this audience of 12 jury members and a bunch of spectators. I was in my T.O. mode, and I was hoping that they had their popcorn ready for what I was about to say. "You know your honor. Throughout this entire court case, you haven't looked me or my attorney in the eye once. It's obvious you're not here in the search for justice, so therefore, there's no point in me asking for a lighter sentence. I don't care what you do cause you're not respecting us. This is not a court of law as far as I'm concerned. No justice is being served here and you still can't look me in the eye. So, I say, do what you wanna do. Give me whatever time you want. Because, I'm not in your hands. I'm in God's hands." Only the two black jurors in the courtroom probably understood what was just said, because the family of the victim had no clue, nor did anyone else. The judge took a deep breath, removed the spectacles from his face and looked dead at me. "Mr. King." The judge paused, as he took another deep breath and began to lightly tap his finger-nails along his stand. "Let me for a minute talk to you not as the judge presiding over your case. Nah. Not right now. I'm going to talk to you as Theodis Brown," as he pointed his glasses towards me. "This is Theodis. Theo as they called me growing up. Neo Theo more so cause all my grandma seemed to buy me were bright colored clothes. See you're probably looking at me in one of two ways. One could be he's a black judge, so he understands the game. And in a way you're right. Black men are more likely to get unfair sentences. Black men are more likely to be targeted by law enforcement. So on and so on. If you are thinking that, then you are correct. You could also be looking at me saying he don't know nothing about the struggle. He has his robe, gets called your honor, probably has a wall full of degrees all in his home. Hell, he even a black judge, living in Montana. And yes, you're right about part of that, if that is what you're thinking. But, what you probably didn't think I knew was that what you just said weren't your own words. See you see the grey hairs and the glasses, and assume that a 63-year-old brother don't know about this young boy shit. And courtroom, excuse my language right now. This is the man, not the judge talking. But, let me say a little something to you right now. Now the baby's in the trash heap balling. Momma can't help her, but it hurts to hear her calling. Brenda wants to run away, momma say you making me lose pay and social workers here every day. Now Brenda's gotta make her own way. Can't go to her family, they won't let her stay. No money no babysitter, she couldn't keep a job. She tried to sell crack but end up getting robbed. So now what's next, there ain't nothing left to sell. So she sees sex as a way of leaving hell. It's paying the rent, so she really can't complain. Prostitute found slain, and Brenda's her name, she's got a baby." The courtroom was already quiet, but I swear you could hear a centipede crawling in between the walls right now. "That Tupac you just spit Mr. King, comes from the same Tupac that went to performing arts school in my city. That's right. I'm Baltimore born and bred. Since my mama dropped me off in '55 in Lafayette. Yeah, I see you raising your eyebrows as if you know. Tyrone 'Muggsy' Bogues and those Dunbar boys. Raised in the same hood. You see I look like an old man who is out of touch. But son, I was dancing to hip hop before you were a speck in God's eye, so don't you dare try to plagiarize someone else's words in my courtroom. You not him. You Darnell Preston King. I grew up in the same type of environment as Pac, yet I went a different way. My mama had me at 17. And just like Brenda, she put my black ass in a trash can. She put me in the trash and she died the same way. In the trash, stabbed up. I watched my grandmother, who had already raised five children of her own, struggle and scrape so I could have clothes on my back, food on the damn table and a roof to sleep under. It was a leaky roof most of the time, but nonetheless, it was a roof. I had to fight for my shoes and my clothes. I stole at times. I ran from police. However, I grew up and didn't let my circumstances define me. **I DEFINED!!!**," as he pointed to himself. "Who I am. I believe that everything you do bad comes back to you tenfold. So, everything that I did that was bad back in my day, I suffered for it. But in my heart, I believe what I'm doing now is right. So, I feel like I'm going to heaven. I know I messed it up, but

3

he said something along those lines in his last interview in the '96 VIBE issue. I was in my 40's at the time. Oh yeah. I know the game and I know what it's like. The difference is I learned before I had to learn. And you gone learn today." The courtroom was literally in a state of shock. No one had ever heard a judge speak like this. And quite frankly, it was something no one would ever think would occur in a courtroom. "For the crime of simple assault with the intent to cause bodily harm. Mr. King, I hereby sentence you to six months' probation, 1000 hours of community service and you will pay a fine of $500."

"**OH, THIS IS BULLSHIT!!!**," the victim's father said, as he stormed out the courtroom. I simply looked around and blew a breath of relief, happy that I didn't have to do any jail time for simply punching a drunk white boy in the face. As Judge Brown got up and exited the courthouse, I gave no fight as court officers escorted me and my attorney out of the courtroom. I simply glanced at the walls, totally ignoring the chatter that was going on within the building, which was a lot. With a pat on the back from my legal counsel, we whisked away through the doors, hoping to never have to see this place again. This was a huge case for my life. Trust, it had nothing to do with me gaining some kind of clout by spending a portion of my life inside of a prison. Hell, we all knew about prison and how nutty it was inside of those walls. The whole fact was that this incident occurred in the state of Montana, way outside the comfort of black folks and I had a flipping black judge. It was like all the stars aligned for me and me only.

Man sometimes, you just gotta chalk things up to luck and luck only.

TRUTH SESSION #1

"MAN IS Y'ALL OVERLY WOKE ASS, PREDATOR LOCS HAVIN ASSES REALLY THAT MAD OVER BLACK PAN-THER???!!! CAN Y'ALL PLEASE SHUT THE FUCK UP WITH THIS SHIT???!!!" Those two young bucks were looking at me, shook from the thunder that was in my voice and the lightning that clicked with each word I said. I was much older than both of these clowns, much wiser and outright bigger than both of their skinny bodies combined. You try to enlighten the younger generation, but sometimes, they thought they knew it all. I couldn't really blame them, because it was a time when I was their age, and I thought I knew it all as well. These boys might have considered themselves woke, but I sincerely hoped they weren't thinking about raising up on me, cause they both knew that I would put their woke asses to sleep. "Old timer look," said Rahman, adjusting the tie under his vest. "You kill me man. You wonder why we in here talking about this. Let me ask you something. Serious question. With all due respect to the time you have spent here on mother earth. How is this movie uplifting the black race? How is this liberating us?

How is a bunch of brothers and sisters going to a movie theatre in some African garb freeing us? Huh? Like serious question." I had to laugh to keep from cursing. This smug look came across my face as I started to shift my eyes between Rahman and Ra. "Hold on y'all," I told 'em. I had to head into the kitchen to get me a drink, because I see where this conversation was about to go. "And you need to stop calling your brothers niggas man. It's not cool at all," Ra said from the couch. "You right youngin'. You right." I came back in the living room after retrieving a pop from the fridge. "Y'all ain't niggas. Y'all are two ignat muthafuckas wrapped up in black skin. Man look. The funny shit is that part of the movie talked about negativity, and you two hotep ass, dashiki mountain top ass boys embracing that right now. Look here man," as I took me a seat on the adjacent couch. "You wanna know what I saw. I saw a nearly all black cast. Some great brothers in Chad and Mike. **MUTHA-FUCKING KILLMONGER!!!** Bury me in the ocean with my ancestors who jumped from ships, because they knew that death was better than bondage. That was some powerful shit. **I SAW BEAUTIFUL BLACK SISTERS!!!** What's the last movie where you saw that much fine African ass on one screen and they weren't in a strip club? You had women with long hair, short hair, grey hair. Hell, a lot of 'em were bald and sexier than the damn sisters who had hair. I'd hit a few of 'em from the back and rub that crystal ball hoping that a genie pops out and grant me three wishes. Any who. I saw a million great messages, and all you two can do is be mad and try to give a history lesson. I saw black folks gathered together as one, and no one was fighting over what colors somebody was wearing or the way they had their hat broke off. I saw all that shit. Now, let me be real. It's only three types of people that's mad at this. One, the no pussy getting ass brothers. And truth be told, I ain't never seen naan one of y'all with a female since y'all first introduced y'all selves to me. With all that ass in the film, shouldn't no brother be mad at all. Or, if y'all some take it in the booty ass dudes, do what you do. I understand and don't knock ya. Hey, do ya thang. Two, y'all just some ol' angry ass all the time brothers. Like, c'mon my dude. Why are y'all angry all the damn time? Is life that bad? Does someone key your car every time you go to the gas station? If the Sun comes up, are you mad it ain't Jupiter? I understood brothers in the penitentiary being mad cause they locked down in a cage. However, y'all free and stay mad at dumb shit. Bruh. I've seen enough grumpy old men in my day. I damn sure don't need to see two grumpy young negros. And three, y'all just what I called you two earlier. Overly woke ass brothers. It's a movie. **A FUCKING MOVIE!!!** It embraced a lot. And brothers like y'all, instead of saying damn, good job, you wanna give history lessons and shit. Criticize everyone. You ain't spent one dime to make your own shit, but everything is wrong because the story wasn't told how y'all wanted it to be told. Well, from big homey to you two little marks. Fuck both of y'all. And neither one of y'all gone whoop my ass, so I ain't worried." I took another swig of this fire ass A&W and started flipping through the television while Rahman and Ra sat on the couch, staring at me, not knowing what to say. "That's the problem," I told 'em. "Y'all brothers get these google degrees in history, grow some dreads and think you the savior of the fucking race. I see y'all looking out the corner of my eye. I'm waiting for one of y'all asses to try me. I'll put y'all overly woke asses to sleep, and then you can pray to Muhammed, Allah, Buddha, Jehovah Jireh or even Menkaure to wake y'all the fuck up. Y'all know who that is?" Both of them looked at each other with a confused look while I took another swig of the pop. "Nah. What? Y'all overly woke asses don't know. Here, let me explain. Matter fact, nah. Go research. Give y'all boys something to do. Matter fact, fuck this. Let me get up out of here. I gotta go to my meeting. Ol' fake ass hotep warriors. And fix ya ties. What that say about y'all pop tart asses?" I walked down the hall, letting out a little chuckle, straight into their mama Dora's room. From the time she introduced me to her boys, we became like family. She always provided a meal, a roof, guidance, an ear, whatever I needed.

"Hey Dora. I'm heading out."

"I hear you spazzed out in that living room."

"Hey, really. I'm sorry. I know cursing in ya house ain't allowed and I was just trying to break some things down to your boys that's all." She put her hand in the air and stopped me from talking anymore. "Nah nah. This time. It's okay baby. They needed to hear that shit. I love my boys, but I tell 'em that a man in a white tee and jeans can be smarter and more knowledgeable than one in a bow tie. Dress don't make the man. Enjoy ya meeting baby. And call more often. You know I get worried about you." I smiled at her. "I will Dora. I will. Take care." I walked back towards the living room, mean mugging her sons on the way out. They just sat there. Not doing or saying anything. I grabbed my coat and headed out into this bitterly cold Midwest air. I shut the door, then I remembered that

8

I had one more thing to tell those two knuckleheads. I flung the door back open. "And really. Calm the hell down. Y'all in North Dakota. Ain't nothing but a speck of black out here. You say y'all woke. Then take y'all asses to Chicago and see can y'all wake them goons up on the Southside. The Westside. Y'all ain't doing nothing here trying to preach to a bunch of white people. You wake up them Vice Lords and GD's. You go to California. Wake up those Bloods and Crips. Then and only then have you showed me something. Until then, you ain't showed me nothing. Prove it to yourself." They said nothing back and I shut the door behind me, heading down the steps.

———————————

"I have a question for you all and I need a no filter, straight chaser answer. Tell me, in your own words. What is the square root of truth?" The whole room was about as silent as fans at a Lakers game when The Black Mamba went down. Or better yet, Falcons fans after they blew that 25-point lead in the Super Bowl. I paused myself, mentally, trying to think of my own logical explanation for this one. As I gazed around this circle of men, I saw that the brothers in here were also thinking the exact same thing. Byron, he was fresh out after doing a two-year bid on some distribution charges. The look that he had in his eyes was if he were still high as a kite from the same weed he once sold on the blocks of Beaumont, Texas. Lamont, he had been out for some time now, but that's only after he played double dutch with the prison system for about 20 something odd years. He was the prime example of why we needed fathers in the home. A mama can do all she can, but she can't make a man out of a boy. Only a male figure can do that. Antwon, he was young and wild, but you could tell that he had some upside to him. He was only 20 and hadn't seen the big house. He did however play with the juvenile system a few times. The last time he went in at 17, it was for petty theft. The judge had let him know that his next charge would be as an adult and juvenile couldn't apply. This program was his only means of trying to stay on the straight and narrow. Cleavon. Oh Cleavon. This man was a Triple OG in the streets. He did a smooth 17-year bid starting from when he was 24. At 41, he was released and entered into an entirely different world. 1999 seemed so long ago. That was the year of the Columbine massacre and Amadou Diallo in New York City. What was crazy is that it was damn near the end of March 2018 and white kids were shooting up more schools than ever. Black men were now getting slaughtered by the police in record numbers. Looking at Cleavon now, teaching and trying to impact us mentally, at the tender age of 60, it was hard to see him as a once wild man running the streets of Chicago. Kelvin was last brother in the group. He was 30, but he looked damn near 70. That heroin had really done him in bad. He got hooked on it at 15 years old when he first shot up behind his high school in East Atlanta, Georgia. He rocked back and forth in the chair, scaring me in the process. He made me think of all the crazy movies with that one nutty person who would end up taking your soul like Shang Tsung in Mortal Kombat. This was our getaway from the real world. It was our chance to just be free and face our demons.

"Darnell?"

"Yes sir," I responded to Cleavon. "Tell me what you think," as his head lowered, glasses tilting halfway off of his face. "I don't know Cleavon. I can't give you an answer to that." He stared at me for the next six to seven seconds and placed his glasses back up on his face. "Byron? Twon? Kelvin? Lamont? Can any of you tell me the answer to the question?" Silence continued to echo within the walls as we were all stuck in time, trying to figure out what he was getting at. "Well since everyone has their lips sewn shut tonight and quieter than a porn star without a dick in her, I won't waste any more time. I will, however, challenge you all. I've got five envelopes here on this table in front of you. I figured none of you could give me the answer I needed, so I will make you find the answer. I'm gonna give you two weeks and two weeks only. At one future meeting, and I ain't gone say which one, you all will have the same answer. Are there any questions?" Kelvin raised his hands nervously, trembling as he shook back and forth, the result of his addiction over the years. "M..M..M..Mr. Thomas. I..I..I..du..du..dunno if I'm gone see nex...nex..next week. Let alone Wed..Wed..Wednesday."

"Look at your mother behind you Kelvin?," Cleavon said. "Look at her. You see that woman? She's been making sure that you were gonna make it through all of your days since she didn't give up on you after all those nights that you put her through hell. Breaking into her house. Stealing money and God knows what else. If it was me, your ass would've been gone faster than Lebron when he hauled ass outta Cleveland the first time. However, that's a woman. A mother.

And if a mother doesn't have anything else in this world, she has a bond with her son. She pushed ya ass out. How many hours of labor Debra?"

"33."

"33 hours of *** damn labor Kelvin. 33 fucking hours. **SHE LOVE YOU!!!**" Cleavon then paused and just stared a hole through Kelvin as he continued to tremble, even with his mother's hand on his shoulder, reassuring him that it would be okay. "Gentlemen," he said so calmly, putting his glasses back on. "Until next Tuesday at the same time. Darnell, lock up the room will ya? I gotta go home and warm up my oxtails." We got up to put our chairs away, making small conversation along the way. This was my Tuesday night for the last nine months. Myself and a bunch of other ex-felons coming together to uplift each other instead of tearing the community down. That's what got our asses locked up in the first place. Well, most of us. Stupid decisions. One by one, the fellas filed out the room. Me, I stayed around for a little while longer, reading a few pages from "*The Autobiography of Malcolm X.*" By Any Means Necessary he quoted. He intrigued me. He had fire in his eyes and spoke with authority. Be mad at me all you want, but that sounded like the human version of God to me. They said God, Allah or whatever you wanted to call him had fire in his eyes. When he spoke, even the fish at the lowest depths of the sea would tremble. I truly believe God came back, died in 1965 and left us for a whole lot longer. However, I never looked for the next black leader. I thought that was a major problem with us. Instead of looking in the mirror and playing our part, we looked for someone else to solve the problem because we were too chicken shit to take the bullet. I locked up the room about a half hour after the meeting had ended and headed out. I made sure to zip my coat up and bundle up heavy, as the North Dakota snow up here would kill your vibe to say the least. Yeah, I said that right too by the way. North Dakota. I wasn't bullshittin' when I was talking to the boys. This wouldn't be the first place you think of a black man staying, but we were everywhere, even if America didn't want us there. I braced myself for the initial sting as I walked out the door. "**MAN, IT'S COLDER THAN PENGUIN NIPPLES!!! SHIT!!!**," I shouted out loud. The snow was coming down and it had an agenda against me for all the wrong I had done in my life. Finally, I managed to fight through the slush and make it to my car. I just sat there for a good minute, enjoying the not so cold, yet still destructive chill that was inside my Chevy. I damn near struggled lifting my hand up to put the key in the ignition. As I started the whip up, I cranked the heat up to Venus. I sat there feeling like an icicle until the car actually started to warm up. I only lived three blocks from here, but these road conditions made it seem like three miles. As I savored this heat and let the engine purr, I did what I always did before I left this place, and that was pray. I thanked the Lord above for moving me far away from where I once was. For once in my life, I was into something more powerful than the lure of the crazy life that included fast lights, fast money and fast women. I still had a long way to go, seeing that I was only out of the joint for a little under a year. I had no plans on going back, or ever returning to the lifestyle that got me there. "**DARNELL MAN!!! DARNELL!!!**" I jumped back as I seen someone beating on my window. The snow made it difficult to see who it was and my instinct told me to grab the illegally possessed pistol that was underneath my seat. "**ANTWON!!!**," I shouted through the car window before letting it down a tad bit.

"What the hell wrong with you man? You lucky I ain't shoot yo young ass."

"I'm sorry OG. Man, I'm sorry. But my mom didn't show up. Can you please, and I mean please give me a ride to my house?" I had a serious decision to make. I was only three blocks away from the house. This boy, however, lived on the other side of town. It was four degrees outside with a wind chill of -18. "I tell you what Twon. You can stay at my house tonight and relax, because my black ass ain't driving twenty muthafuckin minutes out of the way in this weather."

"**THANK YOU OG!!! THANK YOU!!!**," as he hurried over to the passenger side of the car and got in. "Man, I thought I was crap outta luck tonight."

"You were if it had been five minutes later," I told him. We slowly pulled away from the center and made the short drive to my modest one-bedroom apartment. I didn't have much, but I was grateful. I moved up here from upstate Portland after my release. I had a stash in a good place back there in Rip City that was just enough to hold me over for a few weeks. Contrary to what they say about the local dope dealer, some of them are good for something besides selling death. A homey holding ya bread down while you gone for some time is something major. I got a job working as a mechanic up here. The shop itself was ran by an ex-felon who had opened up a shop after years of struggling and grinding from one

14

city to the next. It wasn't much to brag on, but it was mines and mines alone. I was 38 years old. No kids, no wife, none of that. "Man OG, this nice up in here." I looked at him like he was plum crazy. "You just talking. This ain't nice, but it will darn sure do for now. Its four walls and a ceiling." I put my bag down and sat down in my makeshift dining room, which was nothing but a picnic table placed at the end of my small kitchen. Twon came and sat down with me. "You hungry man? I got leftover spaghetti in the fridge." "I'll take it," he said. "You gone call yo mama and let her know where you at?"

"Naw. Not right now. I at least wanna warm up first and eat. Plus, sometimes, I don't even think she cares." I listened to him while I made our plates and put 'em in the oven to warm up, because I didn't have a microwave. I grabbed a half consumed can of pop from the fridge and sat back down with him. "Twon, your mother does care. She just doesn't care for the constant array of hurt that you put her through. You see a mother will never waver on her son. Ever. A mother is a mother until the very end. Whether that son is a multi-millionaire or a zoo janitor that scoops up elephant shit for a living, she will always be a mother. See in your case, it was a single mother. God only knows that she went to the moon and back to see you have a chance at life. If she didn't care, she wouldn't have moved y'all outta Soundview Projects in New York and out here to Fargo. Mothers, and good mothers especially, wanna see their kids grow up better than they did. Even if it takes them a little while." I plowed back this now flat ass can of A&W and just looked at Twon sitting with his arms folded at the table. "So, where's your mother?" he asked me. I paused and thought about it for a second.

"DARNELL PRESCOTT KING!!! GET IN HERE AND CLEAN UP THIS PIGSTY OF A ROOM!!!" I hated when my mama just randomly crept in my room and became a drill sergeant from the Marine Corps. "Mom it's fine," as I entered the room. "Boy don't tell me this room is fine. It looks like a damn tornado done ran through this room, circled back like it forgot something and did more destruction. Now clean it up. I'll be back in 30 minutes. Be ready for inspection." She walked out of my room and I just began to cuss her ass out under my breath. I wasn't stupid enough to air my frustrations out loud. I had a black mama. Black mamas will back hand you so quick for mouthing off. Low tone mumbling was the best and only option for me. I hated this life. I really did. I had two parents, both in the Marines. Both of them were strict as all to be damned. Everything I did was based on what they learned in the military. My dad would sometimes pull clothes out of my drawers because I didn't fold them to military standards. My mama used that retarded ass military way of telling time. She would tell me sometimes to be in the house by twenty hundred. I was just wondering what was so hard that she couldn't say eight o'clock. Deep down, I hated growing up in a military family. We lived at Camp Lejeune in North Carolina. I was 14 and on my way to high school the next year. My dad, he was deployed somewhere over in Africa. Djibouti was the place I believe. I think he was working security or something

16

like that. Moms was here, but she couldn't pull away from her mentality of being a drill sergeant last year at Parris Island in South Carolina. She would always tell her friends that she was raising a future Marine and I would respond in my head with "You can kiss my black ass." Again, I only said it in my head, not my actual mouth. I had a black mama, and black mamas will slap the dog pis out of you in a hurry. Not to mention she was born and raised in North Memphis, so she was known to be nutty like the rest of them folks up there. This was my life in a nutshell. All was strict and sheltered, until I hit 18 and graduated high school. I decided to attend college because the picture they painted of the military was one that I refused to let hang on my wall. To their dismay, I used their GI Bill to head out west to the University of Montana. They wanted to be close so they could come and visit, but I had other plans. I wanted to move as far away as possible and meet people in a foreign land that I wasn't accustomed to. Most of all, I wanted to challenge myself in ways that I had never been challenged before. The day I stepped foot in Missoula, Montana was the day my life turned upside down. It wasn't in a bad way as you would expect. It was more so like the wakeup call of wake-up calls. First off, there was the scenery. I mean, the mountains and the lakes did something to me. It put me in a state of peace that I had never before experienced in my life whatsoever. Next, there weren't any military folks around here. I mean none. All my life it was "My dad is a Master Gunnery Sergeant," or "My mommy is a hospital corpsman." I was truly tired of all of that and gave two fucks. For once in my life, I could possibly hear someone say "My mama was a stripper" and I would be absolutely fine with it. I know it wasn't the best of occupations to brag on or have, but it would be refreshing to hear. Lastly, it was just the overwhelming amount of white people. Crazy how I would find that as something amazing right? I stood out, but as my pops told me when going over his military escapades. When you're a brother, they flock to you. Oh yeah. I was indeed ready for that.

I got up and opened the oven to get our plates. "**AHH MAN!!!**," I yelled, reaching in grabbing the hot porcelain. Twon was cracking up at the table. I wanted to choke him, but I couldn't. I was the dumb cluck nut for not putting on the oven mitts before I reached in there.

"You got old timers already I see huh?"

"You mean Alzheimer's little dude?," as I let my right hand sit under the cold tap water of the sink.

"Old timers, Alzheimer's, forgetting things that's completely common sense, whatever you wanna call it. Even I know that you grab a towel or something."

"Well then you bring your ass over here and get it." Twon got up, grabbed the dish towel and put each plate on the stove top. He then reached into the cabinet and grabbed two other plates.

"The hell you doing man? You trying to dirty up all my dishes?"

"C'mon OG. Cool plate under the hot plate. That way I can carry it over without the mitts. Duh." He was being funny as he picked up the joints and sat 'em on the table one by one. I finished running my hand under the water and cut the sink off. It was red, but not blistering or anything so that was good.

"Where's your forks OG?"

"In that red cup right there on top of the refrigerator." He looked at the fridge and then looked back at me.

"Why you keep forks on top of the fridge in a cup?"

"Look," I said sternly. "Do you wanna eat and sleep? Or do you wanna have your tail starve tonight and walk home? Either way, I don't care." "Sorry OG," he said. "I wasn't trying to be rude. Just saying. I ain't never seen anything like that."

"Well now you have," I replied. "Now get two forks so we can enjoy this meal." I was pissed at this point. He got two forks and we began to eat. Things were quiet for the most part. I didn't like quiet, but I know the kid was kind of scared to talk to me due to how I snapped on him. After about five minutes, I couldn't take it anymore.

"Look, I'm sorry. I really am. I shouldn't have gone off on you like that.

I just don't like people talking about my house. You know I'm 38 years old.

Ain't no 38-year-old supposed to be living like this at this age."

"I never judged you," he replied. "I actually thought it was kind of cool that you had metal forks. I just never saw them in a red cup on top of the fridge."

"So, tell me about yourself Twon? What don't I know? It's looking like forks are striking a cord with you." He took another two bites of the spaghetti, looking like I had hit a sore spot in his soul. "I don't like to talk about my past too much, but I never seen metal anything until I was staying in a juvenile hall. Before then, all I knew was plastic forks and spoons. Soundview is hard OG. My mom was a single mom, doing what she could. I didn't have the luxury of wearing Jordan's and Adidas. Cats had Air Nikes. I had air sikes. My clothes were tattered and torn at times. Hell, I used to get into so many fights because the kids on the block would say some ridiculous things to me. Yo son what the heck you got on? Yo B, I wouldn't waste my time robbing you. Look at ya shit yo. Only thing I could get off you son is a towel to wipe my car clean. And the latter was the older cats saying that shit to me. We were poor man. I was there all my life. Looking at dead bodies in the hallways, sleeping on just a mattress, having dreams of making it to the bright lights of Manhattan. I walk to the store and it was always groups of grown men laughing at me. Roasting the hell outta me OG. I mean, wouldn't you get tired of it? I learned early in life that life is checkers, not chess, but everyone turns it into a game that they really don't wanna play. So, when moms finally afforded to pack us up to head out here at 13, I figured I'd be that checkers piece. I didn't give a chance for these cats out here to figure me out. I got out here and became Billy bad ass. You know. In checkers, it's simple. One piece black. One piece red. Jump one before they jump you. I got the jump on all of 'em. I was from New York son. Toughest place on earth B. They ain't give a hoot about fashion or status out here, but they figured I did. I didn't have to bully anyone. All I had to do was give an order to get something done for me and it was done.

I was like a high school Tony Montana."

"And where did it take you?," I asked him.

"To places I never wanted to see. To people that I never wanted to be around. I'm stuck with nothing, trying to earn a GED. I'm trying to make my mother proud. I'm 20 years old with no plan for the future. I mean, I'm trying." I took a bite of my spaghetti, trying to understand this kid as much as I could. I couldn't relate to growing up in a high-rise project building, seeing that I always had the security of military housing. What I could do was relate to him in the only way we were relatable. Our circumstances made us wanna get out and separate from what we had known all of our lives. "Twon, I put it like this. At least you're 20 and still young. You still got time to recover and bounce back. You got your whole life ahead of you. Me, not so much. I just have to make do with what I have and hope that I can obtain more. I'll tell you what. Every Tuesday night, we'll sit at this dinner table after our sessions with the brothers and we'll talk. We will talk about whatever. It doesn't matter. But, but, we will come up with a goal plan for your life and how to achieve them."

"What about you?," he asked. I took a deep breath.

"For me, my life is pretty much stuck in a nutshell. I don't wanna see you go down my path. Gone clean up and chill. You can sleep in my bed tonight."

"You sure OG? I mean I can't come in your crib putting my feet on your couch yo?" I turned back around to look at him as I was scraping the plates into the trash. "It's your house too as long as I'm here." A look of calm rose on his face as if he had for once in his life found trust in someone. Even if he did, I still didn't trust him. He was a good kid from what I had known about him, but it takes me a while to get close to folks, seeing how humans have this uncanny knack of flipping on you with the quickness. However, I God honestly saw something in him. I went to the shower and cut the water on hot. I needed it seeing how cold it was outside and how the heat barely even kept things kosher in here. As the water hit my body, I analyzed all of my tattoos. All 19 of 'em. Down my arms and across my chest, my body was marked up like the subway in Harlem. I closed my eyes just to let the water run over my head. My college days in Missoula, Montana started to play back in my mind.

"So, are you on the football team?" I stopped mid bite in the cafeteria. This random white girl just plopped down at my lunch table and asked me that random question. As I took a glance across the lunch room, I saw three of her friends obviously looking. She either mustered up the courage to speak to me or came over here on a dare.

"Naw. I don't. I just came out here for something different."

"Tracy," as she stuck her hand out.

"D.P.," I replied back, meeting her hand with mines.

"Well look, I'm not going to keep interrupting you, but can you call me sometimes?" She handed me her number on a piece of paper, which was weird because I hadn't saw that shit done since I left high school back the year before. Now one thing that my mama always told me was that if it's too easy, then it ain't worth it. This was looking too easy, but I didn't wanna jump to any conclusions. I was a black speck in a white world, so I was even more cautious. "Yeah sure," I replied. I put her number in my pocket and kept eating as she walked back to the table with her girls, snickering and giggling. I guess they had caught them their token black dude. This reminded me of the scene in the movie He Got Game where Chic had Jesus at the table eating, and Molly and all of her girls came over. They lucky I wasn't in that movie. I would've popped that Molly and been playing for Tech U, specifically for the assistant coaches. I went back to my dorm that crispy fall day and relaxed. I didn't have my next class until 5 p.m. and studying wasn't on my agenda today. I had been in college for a few weeks now. The football team was undefeated at 4-0. Tomorrow was their huge game with fellow Big Sky rival Eastern Washington. I was gonna be there and thoroughly enjoy what the weekend had to offer. I chilled in my twin sized bed playing games on my phone 'til the door swung open. "Man, you better raise yo ass up." Lance smacked me on my shoe. "What's good mane?," I asked him. "Man, there you go with that mane shit. Y'all Carolina niggas are a trip cuz." I gotta good laugh outta dude. Lance Harper was the university's 6'3 all everything player. He played on both sides of the ball. Wide receiver on offense, cornerback on defense and kick returner on special teams. He even played on the school's basketball team, playing the role of their Julius Peppers. He came outta Long Beach Poly, a place where football legends seemed to be birthed at. He kind of reminded me of Deshawn Jackson. "So y'all getting that dub tomorrow night, or do I gotta come out there and show y'all how it's done?" He turned around giving me that negro please look from his desk in the room. "Man please. Are we ready? Are you ready to come out for the squad finally?"

"Man, I'll kill y'all. Y'all ain't ready for Carolina boy."

"Shit nigga please. Only thing come outta Carolina is pulled pork and tobacco. Yeah, yeah, y'all got basketball going good. I'll give you that. But then, Indiana murders y'all as far as hoops goes, so y'all really ain't the kings of that shit. So, when it comes to football, like I said, nigga please." "**WHAT???!!!**," I yelled to him. "Indiana. Man, who the hell done came outta Indiana? Where the fuck is Indiana while I'm asking?"

"Umm bruh, for the longest they had the only single class tourney going. If they ever change it, it's because 49 other states made an ass ton of money and they wanna follow suit. I thought we balled in Cali. That was until I took a summer trip out there to see some of my relly's. Man, those Indiana dudes got basketball hoops everywhere. The playground, the park, the gas station, in the middle of the cornfield, at the funeral home. You name the place and they got it there. They live and breathe that shit man. Look up East Chicago Roosevelt and East Chicago Washington from 1970 and 71. Look up Shawn Kemp, Z-Bo Randolph, Larry Legend, Oscar Robertson, Glenn Robinson, look 'em all up. Hell, I got two words for you. John Wooden. Hell, he came out to Cali and had niggas win eleven of 'em at UCLA cuz. Man y'all ain't fucking with that state when it comes to basketball or history."

"**MICHAEL JORDAN!!!**," I yelled out. "Great, y'all got one. Now keep going." I began to ramble off the many legends that came out of my state. I started naming cats we had play for our college hoop squads who weren't from Carolina, cause they wanted to come and play where the legends played. He had me in the end, but it was still fuck Indiana basketball. I was Tar Heel blue 'til I was six feet under. And with that said, fuck Duke as well. We chilled out for a bit until Lance went off to practice later in the day and I started to get ready for my final class of the week. I was far from what you would call a mathematician, but economics was one of my prerequisite courses for my major in Nutritional Science. Now what did math have to do with trying to help folks physically and keep them healthy? I had no clue to tell you the truth. All I knew was that I wanted to do whatever it took to be training people one day so they could become the biggest, baddest and best human specimen alive. As I departed through my dorm building, the sounds of loud music blaring through the halls killed my ear drums. Most of the campus was already done with classes for the week and partying it up as they prepared for the big game tomorrow. It wasn't bad being out here in a foreign land not known by anyone. It was actually quite invigorating. As I sat in class that night, I took notes, but also jotted down the goals that I had wished to obtain throughout my life.

1. Graduate with a bachelors in nutritional science

2. Start occupation as a strength coach at an elite university

3. Have kids and get married

Those were the three main goals for my life. My parents had lived theirs and it was time to live mines. After surviving the two hours bore session from my professor, I went back to the dorm to see the whole building lit up in a party atmosphere that I hadn't ever seen before. Everyone in the damn state was here it seemed. I just wanted to make it back to my room. "Hey, you?," as I felt a tug on my arm. I turned back to see it was Tracy holding a beer in her hand. She looked pretty wasted.

"Sup beautiful?"

"So, umm. You didn't call me."

"I'm sorry yo. Just honestly forgot you know. School and shit."

"Well, will you forget about me now?" Just then, she dropped her breasts out of her shirt. I knew she was wasted and all, but she had some nice C cups. "Woo, umm, yeah. I'm gone head to my dorm room."

"So, can I come?," she said, ever so slurred. "Naw, you good." She rolled her eyes and turned away from me, oblivious to the fact that her breasts were still sticking out. From the screams I heard down the hall, I could tell that everyone else had seen them now. All pussy ain't good pussy. I had learned in my time through observation that white chick, black dude and alcohol equals rape charge. It wasn't happening to me. As Eddie Griffin once said. Ask O.J. Ask Kobe. Tiger Woods, it ain't no good.

I settled back in my room, probably the only student who wasn't living it up outside in the halls. "**FUCK THOSE FAG-GAT BIRD BITCHES!!!**" Some crazy white dude yelled it in the hallway. How did I know it was a white boy you ask?

Only white boys shout WOOO after making a statement like that. From the sounds of it, there were a bunch of Ric Flair imitators out there. All I needed to hear was a space mountain reference and the night would be complete. "**BITCH COME HERE AND RIDE SPACE MOUNTAIN!!!**" And right on cue, there it was. I threw on my headphones and cranked up some Nas. 1996 through 1998 were the years of the magician as I called it. It seemed like those three years in hip hop had transcended any era that ever came before it. The Fugees dropped The Score. Reasonable Doubt was dropped by Jigga Man. Ghostface dropped Ironman and UGK's Ridin Dirty was simply before it's time. And, that was just '96. 97 saw its own fair share of greatness with Camp Lo dropping an underrated classic in Uptown Saturday Night, and Wu-Tang dropping WuTang Forever, with its lead single Triumph containing the greatest introductory verse of any song in hip hop history. Lastly, 98 was my personal favorite, simply because of The Miseducation of Lauryn Hill. No disrespect to any other group or artist who dropped that year, like Outkast with Aquemini. However, Lauryn made an all-time culture classic. I mean you couldn't lose in those years. I sat in my bed, eyes closed, daydreaming about the day I would make it out on my own. Not as a teenager, but as a grown ass man.

I got out of the shower and headed to my room. As I did, I saw Twon sprawled out on the couch. "I thought I told you that you could have the bedroom young buck."

"I can't do it OG. It's disrespectful to me so I'm good out here. Can I just get a blanket though?" I hesitated for a minute. "Yeah little bro. Hold on." I walked in my room and shut the door. I sat on the edge of my bed and just started to ball tears. I only had two blankets in my house and they were both on my bed. Now, this wasn't me trying to be selfish towards him, but a grown man should have more than two blankets in his house. The incompleteness of my life started to set in yet again. To Twon, I was someone to look up too. To myself, I was a failure at life. I barely made ends meet and my apartment that I had was next to nothing. The only reason I got it was because of boss man at the mechanic shop. I began to just ponder not even being here. I wasn't a grown man. I was a boy stuck in a man's body. I sucked up my tears and wiped my face clean as I walked back out the room.

"Here you go young brother."

"OG?"

"Yeah," as I hit the fridge for another A&W. "A. I just wanna let you know that this is the first time in my life that I actually felt like I was in a home." I shut the fridge door, holding a full bottle of the most delicious pop ever, cause the can wasn't gonna cut it this time. I walked back into the living room to see what Twon was talking about. "How? Look at what's in here. A beat-up green couch, a mattress, a box spring and a fold out picnic table that's a dinner table."

"**THAT'S IT!!!**," Twon yelled. "Look at that man. That's more than what I ever had in life. You actually have dinner at a table. At a table yo. I never had dinner at a table until tonight. My mama still doesn't have a table to set food out on. Everything is left on the stove. I'm rich right now. Do you get that? You're rich to me." I was taken aback by his words. I never knew that the poor man could be wealthy and the wealthy man could be poor. This kid had a mindset unlike any other. "So, let's do this. There's a store across the street from the house. You wanna brace this cold weather, go get some hot chocolate, and sit at this table and drink?" Twon sat up on the couch. "Yeah. I'm down." I went into the bedroom, throwing on some long johns, a hoodie and some sweats. I know I was just walking across the street, but the wind chill was set to Glacier. We walked outside to see that it had stopped snowing, which was a good thing. I looked up at the sky. Amazing how in the winter time the sky turned an eerie brown. "So, is this as brutal as New York winter's?," I asked him, with my head tucked into my coat. "Naw, not even. This winter isn't brutal. Fargo winters are a cake walk compared to New York joints. At least I got a decent coat here." We squinted at each other through the howling wind. I now started to really feel sympathetic. If the kid didn't have a decent coat during childhood, you could just imagine the pain he felt and I'm not talking about the physical. We made it to the Arab owned convenience store. I shook the chill off of me long enough to find a box of hot chocolate. "$5.75. This damn chocolate better enhance my blood circulation," I said out loud. Everything was more expensive at the little mom and pop joints. I gladly paid for it, though, and politely said thank you. I learned that kindness went a long way in this world. You treat the CEO with the same respect that you treat the janitor. "**ANTWON!!!**," I yelled. "**TWON!!!**"

"Oh, your son is outside waiting for you. I saw him when he walked out," said the cashier. I walked outside and saw him standing there shivering his ass off.

"What you doing out here?"

"I didn't have any money so I didn't wanna seem like I was just tailing off of you."

"You don't have to feel like that young brother," I told him, as we trenched it through the heavy snow on the ground. "I'm not one to look down on someone else." And just as I said look down, I actually looked down to see something had fallen out of Twon's coat as we got back to the front of my apartment building. I bent down to pick it up out of the snow. "Twon what's this?" He was quiet as a church mouse.

"I was still hungry."

"So, you steal two funky packs of fuckin Ramen noodles that cost twenty cents each? Is that what we do? Get yo ass in the house mane." I walked up the steps and turned around to see him still standing in the same spot, right at the gate. "Are you coming inside or are you gonna pity yourself for being less of a man?" He then slouched his way up, looking dumbfounded and sad as if he had lost his dog or something. I waited by the door and smacked him upside the head as he walked in. "Owww OG. Damn. You ain't gotta do all that."

"Well I gotta do something," as I slammed the door behind me. "What is your problem? You put your life on the line for a fuckin twenty cent pack of Ramen noodles. I mean, what were you thinking? They kill young black men for less."

"I dunno," he said. "It's hard not having any money, nor much to go on in life." I wanted to choke the kid, but again,

I understood his pain, so I had to empathize. "Tell you what. Take yo tail over to that stove. I got two pots total in this house. Boil those noodles in one pot and just boil water in the other. They say keep what you kill. So, cook what you steal. Tell me when it's done and I'll come out." He looked at me confused as ever. I walked into my bedroom, closing the door behind me. I grabbed today's paper that I had laid out in there and went looking through the classified section. I was looking for any and every gig I could imagine that could pay me more. The money somewhere had to be better than what I was getting now. Plus, I had a degree. Only thing is that a felon had a hard time being trusted. Then, I saw it. Interviews were being held at North Dakota State University for a trainer position. I started to wonder if football could bring me back to the road of glory.

It was in the fourth quarter. The game was tied 23-23 with 12:47 left. Eastern Washington had just forced us to punt. The atmosphere here was amazing. It was the first collegiate game that I had ever witnessed in my life in person. It may have been D-1AA, but it was big time in my eyes. During the timeout, after the kickoff, is when I really soaked in the atmosphere of where I was at. The student section was beyond hyper as they were still jumping around. I never thought in a million years that I would be somewhere like this, seeing how sheltered my life was coming up on military base after military base. Both teams came out of the timeout looking renewed. Eastern

Washington was starting from its own 37-yard line. The ball was snapped. The QB dropped back and slung it to his slot receiver for a quick slant. It was picked off. I had never in my life heard a crowd erupt the way it did in that moment. We took the lead back 29-23 and this place was rocking. I'm pretty sure an earthquake was being caused from the noise right now and all the snow on the peaks of the Montana mountains had been shaken off. In the end, we held on for a 37-33 victory, with Lance making the game saving interception on third down in the end zone with four seconds to go. I watched as the student section stormed the field. I didn't have any intention on trying to join the mayhem. I simply stood in awe in section 121, more amazed that I was seeing my breath in October. As the dust settled and everyone started to file out, I made my way down by where all the players came out, waiting for Lance. There were parents, friends and all kinds of family out here. They were all so jubilant in this moment. If only I was in that position. And it was right there in that moment that I decided next year, I would be.

———————

"**OG!!!**" I walked out the room and into the kitchen. I saw the nervousness on Twon's face as he had already placed two cups on the table with a huge mixing bowl of noodles in the middle. I really didn't wanna talk to this kid right now for the fowl mistake he made earlier, but I had to let it go. Plus, I had to remember as well that my own wrong decision in life had me in the position that I was in now. "Man, you ain't pour none of the juice out?"

"Well I mean, all I could find was a mixing bowl, so I just poured everything in there."

"No chopped up hot dogs, cracked eggs, none of that."

"Huh?," he said, with a dumbfounded look on his face.

"I thought you were from the projects man. When I used to go visit my grandmother in Memphis, she always cracked an egg in them thangs. Maybe chopped up some hot dogs in 'em too. Bruh, she made a meal out of this. We didn't eat Top Ramen. We ate a five-course dinner with maybe two dollars' worth of food. That's why I had you boil two pots of water. I thought the additives were going in the other pot. I'll take it though. Now, say the prayer." I sat down and bowed my head, just waiting for him to give grace. After about fifteen seconds, I heard nothing. I opened my eyes to see that he was staring dead at me.

"What's the problem?"

"I never prayed a day in my life OG. I don't believe in God."

"Why Not?"

"I mean think about it yo. If there was a God, why is everyone dying in the most messed up ways on this earth? Why are there kids that go hungry every night and have to literally scrape garbage cans to find a meal? They say Jesus was this larger than life type dude who loved everybody. But, if you loved your people, why do you let them suffer?" He was distraught and uncomfortable. I could tell that someone had this conversation with him way before I did.

"So, let me ask you 'Twon. Are you an atheist?"

"What's that?"

"It's one who doesn't believe in God. Are you one of those?"

"I mean, if that's what it's called, I guess. I just don't believe in an imaginary creature sitting on top of a cloud saying that you gone go to hell if you don't believe in me."

"Well, do you believe in anything?" He paused, raising his head to the sky, wandering off as if he were looking at something. Then he bowed his head. "Yo to whoever hears this, keep the food warm, and us tonight, also. Amen. Does that make you happy OG?"

"It ain't about making me happy. Your belief ain't necessarily gotta be my belief. I just wanna know why you said Amen?"

"I mean. I hear everyone else always saying that, so I figured that's how you do it. But then no one really knows where that comes from. They just say the shit." I sipped my hot chocolate, watching him as he dug into his first bite of noodles. "What you mean where it came from?"

"Talking about the term Amen."

"Yeah. That's how you end a prayer."

"Bullsh-. I'm sorry. It came from the Egyptians OG." I scooped up a forkful of noodles and gulped them down.

"Enlighten me professor?"

"I dunno man. Just what I heard. They say everything Christian came from the Egyptians."

"Whatever man. Is the food hitting the spot young buck?"

"Yeah it is."

"Did you call your moms?"

"Naw. I texted her, but she ain't responded back."

"Don't you think you should put some effort into actually making a call? I mean, it is 8:32 at night and she still ain't heard your voice."

"I mean. Moms cool. She knows I'm good. We ain't in New York. We in Fargo. The only bad thing that happens over here is a sheep getting killed on the farm." I got a good laugh out of that line, but it still didn't take my anger away from the situation at hand. "So, let me get this straight," as I slurped a big fork full of noodles. "Your mama works her butt off to get you out here. You go to juvie hall three times in four years. She still has faith in you. You got a roof over your head. You steal from the store, didn't get caught and don't believe in God? At what point do you say it may not be everyone else? It may just be me."

"I never put the blame on anyone else OG."

"But I heard the tone in the way you talked when I asked you about your mom. Deep down, you feel she is responsible. As much as you hated leaving New York, you wanted to stay behind and be one of them. Now you feel like you ain't you, so you gotta steal from a bunch of folks in country North Dakota, all because they don't realize a New Yorker. Why? What do you wanna do in life 'Twon?" He took a huge gulp from his cup. "I never thought about that OG. I mean. I guess I always kind of liked animals. I always liked the thought of being a veterinarian, or something along those lines." That answer shocked me, but it opened my eyes to something even greater. "I'll tell you what. Let's make a deal. Right here, right now. You get your GED. Don't steal, stay home every night, go to the meetings, meet me every Tuesday for dinner and I'll do what I can to get you working around animals, or something of value. And on my end, I'll go over to one of these local schools to apply to be a trainer for the sports teams over there."

"Why you wanna do that? What benefit will I see if you go there and I go to a zoo?"

"It's called pushing son. I push you to be your best and you push me to be mines. Remember, you're never too old to learn and you're never too young to be taught a different way of life." I extended my hand out. With a smile, he grabbed it. "Alright OG. I got this. Rather we got this." We finished up the night eating, laughing, cleaning up the kitchen and such. He went to the living room couch to watch TV on the 27 inch while I took it to the bedroom. As I stared into space, I asked God in that moment to lead me to victory. I had taken too many losses in my life. Now, at almost forty years old, I was ready to obtain a monumental victory like the night Montana beat Eastern Washington when I was in college. I was at my crossroads.

BOOM BOOM BOOM!!! BOOM BOOM BOOM!!! I thought I was dreaming that something was making that loud booming noise. "**OG!!!**," I heard Twon call me from the living room. "**SOMEONE AT THE DOOR!!!**" I got up groggy, feeling the effects of the early morning slouch. I wasn't a morning person at all. If you wanted to see me at my grumpiest, then mess with me when I first wake up. I sat up, reaching for my house shoes, so I could entertain whoever this was messing with me early in the morning. **BOOM BOOM BOOM!!!** "**HOLD UP SHIT!!!**," I yelled. This was beyond irritating now. Passing the clock, I saw it was 9:18. Who was messing with me on my off day? I flung the door open. "Umm ma'am. Can I help you?" She was a small statured sister who stood no more than 5'3. "Yes, you can. Is my son here?" Her funky ass attitude was pissin me off, but I had to keep cool.

"You mean Twon?"

"I mean my son. Where is he?"

"Mom," Twon said, peeking around the half open door.

"Boy get yo ass out of this house and let's go. Had me worried half the damn night about your ass."

"Umm ma'am, let me introduce myself."

"I don't need to know who you are. All I know is that if you ever take my baby again, the coroner will be here present at your place. You understand me?" Those words were followed by a slap. The slap was a mosquito bite to say the least, but it was the principle. This broad really just hit me. My blood began to boil as my fists clenched up. I know I was raised never to hit a woman, but since she was acting like a man, I was damn sure ready to treat her like one. "It's okay OG. It's okay." Twon grabbed his coat and kept me at bay. "I'll go with my mom. Til next time."

"Okay," I whispered, rubbing my jaw, clearly still pissed off from getting slapped. "C'mon boy. Fuck wrong with you?" I watched as she slapped him upside his head what seemed like a million times. His mama was crazy. I shut the door slow and just sat on the couch, trying to subside my anger. I did what I learned to do during hard time, and that was meditate and harness my negativity into something positive. I stayed in this state for about 20 minutes. Through that time, I thought about everything from former inmates that I had bonded with to my mother, father, grandmother, my childhood friends from all over and majority North Carolina. I thought about it all. All except for one. That was my grandfather. I didn't feel bad for the old man. I didn't like to speak ill will of the dead, but he was nothing to me and will forever remain that. He beat on my grandmother, who is no longer with us on this earth, all throughout their relationship. He forced so much dissension between her, my mom and her siblings. He didn't care. He was a raging alcoholic. Two weeks before he passed, my mom brought him down to the house we were staying in on the Marine base. He was in town to visit her. "I love you grandson," he said, as I continued doing work on the computer. "Luh you too," I said. I didn't want him to hear the word love. I wanted him to hear "luh." In my mind, it meant half ass, much like the job he did of raising my mama, auntie and uncles. I gave him a half ass hug on his way out. I didn't care. My grandmother was my world. In my eyes, you hurt my grandmother and I hurt you. And if I couldn't hurt you physically, then I had no care for you in the world. Two weeks from that date, he passed. I had mixed feelings. In one instance, I was glad that he was gone. My people no longer had to look at him and see despair. In another sense, I felt awful for having so much resentment towards the man. Now, you can chalk that up to me being 17 at the time, which usually is accompanied with a don't give a damn about anything mindset. You could also chalk it up as me not being a worthy human being. I started to think the latter. I remember when we got the phone call. I was taking a shit, fresh home from basketball practice. I heard my mom scream. "**MY DADDY JUST DIED!!!**" She kept repeating it over and over.

My father tried his best to comfort her, but it was to no avail. His body was still in the house he was staying at while down here, so we made the twenty-minute drive south of Lejeune. As we entered the house, I could see a few family members from down there gathered up near the bedroom. I walked in there to take a look myself. That lowly January day of 1998 had become even lower. I had no sympathy in my heart. I just looked at him, already swollen up and bloated. I just stared at him and thought about our last interaction. I think that's what hurt the worst. Me seeing him in his last hoorah. I carried this burden with me for quite some time, until I found out later that in his last days at the hospital, he told the family that he ain't apologizing for nothing. Then, I thought to myself, fuck him. Fuck my grandfather. The only grandfather I had was my great grandfather, who was a standup guy to say the least. This one, this one here, fuck him. As far as my father's dad, well, he was gone before I was born, so I never got a chance to meet him. From what I heard about him, however, he was a standup guy as well, doing what he had to do to take care of all his children. Nine to be exact. This grandfather right here, though, fuck him. If I am condemned for having such despise for one man in my life, then fuck it. I forgave him in the end, but when I found out he wasn't willing to be a man and say sorry to everyone else, well in my eyes, his ass could rot for all I care. If I never saw his grave again for all the days in my life, then I would still be good. Long as my mama was good, then I was good. I arose from my meditative state. However, I was no longer thinking about having that anger consume me again. As many negative thoughts I had in that session, I now wanted to smile and tell the old man I love him. It's wild ain't it. With growth comes change in mindset and everything else. David Banner once said "How could I possibly learn more and more every day and not contradict my former thinking?" He was right. By now, I had learned the art and power of letting go. I actually smiled. "Rest easy old man," I said out loud. I rose up for the kitchen and just tried to figure out what I would do with this day. I pulled the remaining ramen noodles out of the refrigerator and heated them up in a skillet with some soy sauce. I poured some frozen veggies in there and cracked an egg in 'em as well. I would at least eat good if nothing else. While they were cooking, I put the leftover spaghetti in a Ziploc bag and froze it. Black folks were good for freezing some shit and thawing it out later. After finishing up my masterpiece of a meal, I went back to the bedroom and saw the newspaper still lying on the floor. The classified section was standing out to me like a sore thumb. "NDSU," I whispered. I had to get there. I didn't wanna waste my time calling. I wanted to be live and in person, so they can see the fire that I had to obtain this job. I took a quick shower and threw on the only nice pair of dress clothes that I had. I also grabbed my folder which contained my credentials, my degree and my felony record. I hurried out the house and started up that beat up Chevy that I had. Hey, it was old, but it was mines, and it got me from point A to point B. I made it to the university athletic office in what seemed to be the blink of an eye. That was impressive considering how much slush was on the ground from last night's snowfall. Winter time in North Dakota wasn't anything nice I tell you. "Hi sir. Can I help you?," said the receptionist at the desk. "Yes

ma'am. I'm here to interview for the strength trainer position."
In my bumbling moment, I dropped my folder and everything.

"I'm sorry ma'am."

"No worries. However, I don't think Dr. Pizar is taking interviews today. Nor is that position open."

"Look. Ma'am? I just drove through this terrible snow to come see about this job. Now, I am not getting smart, but at the least, could you ask him if I could speak with him for maybe five to ten minutes?" The look of desperation was obvious on my face. "One moment please," as she smiled and headed towards a side door. I was more nervous than buffet owners who saw twenty obese people come through the door. "He'll see you now," she told me after the most anxious five minutes of my life. She led me back to his office where I saw the trophies and plaques on the wall. This school had done good in recent times. Repeat NCAA titles in football. A top five quarterback who would light up the NFL for years to come. That's was impressive to say the least. As he continued his phone conversation, he signaled for me to sit down and relax. I waited calmly, now locked in on the degrees that decorated his office walls. Two masters and a PhD. He was truly impressive. "How are you sir?," as he got off the phone.

"Thomas."

"Darnell," as we shook hands.

"So, I hear you are interested in one of our strength coach positions."

"No sir. Interested would be sitting at home, calling you and asking who it will be. Determined would be driving a beat-up Chevy through this weather, coming straight into the director's office and telling him to hire me now, flaws and all, because I'm the best person for this job." He shook his head up and down. "I like it so far. Tell me all about your history." I dropped my packet on the desk. "In here sir, you will find everything about me. I graduated with a bachelor's in Nutritional Science and a minor in Sports Medicine. I also did some time for felony assault. I was at my alma mater watching a game. After the game, a young man recognized me as a former player and started to belittle me about a play in which I cost my team a guaranteed national title. I tried to walk away, but I felt the saliva hit my face. The young man spit on me. When you spit on someone, those are fighting actions. I beat him so bad that he had to drink out of a straw for the next year. I am a flawed man, but I am a man at the same time. I come in here and you have trophies of four straight NCAA titles I see. I just wanted to relish in having one, but I know my mistake took that away, just like that mistake of beating that young punk took years of my life away and many opportunities, because no one trust or wants to hire an ex-felon."

"Stop right there," he said. "Tell me about this play that cost your team the game." He had challenged me to go back to a time in my life that I completely wanted to forget about, but that I had to face constantly in my sleep. I didn't wanna go back, but I had no choice at this moment, because I opened the door.

"So, you sure you wanna be here?," Lance asked me.

"Man, this cake bruh. I had Marine parents. This ain't nothing but a walk in the park compared to the shit my pops used to make me do for punishment."

"Like what?"

"You ever hear of the crucible my dude?"

"Sound like some shit you find in a medieval castle."

"Shit I wish. He didn't take away my N64 or cut off my phone line. I fuck up and he would drive me down to Parris Island and make me do that shit. I'd rather starve."

"So, what the fuck is it? Nigga you still ain't said that shit."

"Just picture dancing with the devil for three days. Only difference is that I got to sleep and didn't touch a gun. I did that shit three times in my life."

"Damn like that G?"

"Like that. Marines are bat shit crazy, and I had two of 'em to deal with." I know Lance was tough, but even civilians knew that Marines went through the most badass boot camp. "Okay. Let me gone head and introduce you to coach." I had never stepped foot on a college football field. It wasn't intimidating to say the least. "**COACH!!! COACH!!!**"

"**YEAH LANCE!!!** Who is this?" He walked me up feverishly.

"Coach, this is my good friend Darnell P. King. He wanna try out." Coach looked at me up and down. "Well kid, you certainly have size. About 220 I assume?"

"213 sir. 6'2 and loves to hit."

"Have you ever played football?"

"No sir. Not besides street football. But I did grow up with Marine parents who sometimes liked to play dig a trench and hide in it for fun. I dunno. It was something my dad liked to do. Oh, and he made me survive the crucible. Like, three times."

"Semper Fidelis. I like you already. I was in the Corps for four years. Lance, take him over to the equipment manager. We'll see what you're made of son. By the way. What does the P stand for in your name?"

"Performance sir."

"Good. Because if you come out here half ass, the players on this team are gonna make it stand for something else. Get my drift?" I shook my head in acknowledgement and followed Lance. Deep down, I was scared to death. I talked a good game a lot, but I was about to go up against college athletes who seemed like they were four times my size when they threw the pads on. Putting on shoulder pads and a helmet seemed damn near like going to war. I remember when my dad would come home and dress me in the young Marine Corps gear. He would put a helmet on my head and give me a fake rifle. He would take me out to a sand pit on base and dig holes. We would act like we were firing on the enemy. As a young child, I thought it was the coolest thing in the world to experience. I was lucky enough not to lose my dad in any major conflicts that the world seemed to always be entrenched in. However, I knew he had the mental scars from some of the stuff he had seen. That probably was the only reason for me to stay back home so that he could have an outlet to escape those thoughts sometimes. I had to be my own man, however, so he completely understood. "**ALRIGHT DUMMY O!!! GIVE 'em A LOOK!!!**" I was off behind the dummy O in line with the rest of the team who wasn't playing. As they lined up, coach blew his whistle. "**KING!!! COME OUT HERE!!!**" I jogged it up to the huddle where coach was. "You know anything about receiver routes son?"

"I know 1 is a slant. 9 is a fade. That's how they usually go."

"Okay, this is what I want. The D is giving a two-safety look. I'm lining up three receivers, you on the strong side. They don't know you and are not gonna respect you. If you want them to respect you, run the post, make the catch and flip into the end zone when you catch it. Got it?"

"Yup."

"Alright guys. Break this huddle. Let's see what they got." As coach left, I listened for the call. "Play action, 65 post. King you know what you got right?"

"Yeah."

"Austin and Houston, y'all know what it is."

"Wait a minute. Time out. Y'all from Texas?," I asked the other two receivers. "Yup. That's how much our daddy loves that state. He named us after the cities we were born in," Austin said. I just shook my head. "**READY, BREAK!!!**" I lined up to the strong side. "Oh shit. We got a baby out here. I'll lineup five off to make you feel special. Don't think you getting any rip on me homey." I completely ignored whoever the hell he was. Lance was on the other side guarding one of the Tex-Mex twins. The ball was snapped and I took off ten yards down the field. As the corner opened up to follow me, I took it out two more yards to appear as if I was running the fade route. He completely bit on it and I made my move to the center of the field. The free safety had drifted up somewhat, so all I needed was the ball to be placed in the right spot. As I turned my head to look for the ball, I could see that I was money. It was me against the world. The ball literally dropped into my hands as if Jesus himself had hand delivered it to me. I took it and cut it upfield, feeling the brush of the corner's hand as he tried to grasp my leg. I heard the screams from the rest of the team as I sprinted towards the goal line. Once I hit the one, I did a front flip into the end zone, followed by a flip of the ball that Randy Moss would've been proud of. I crossed my arms, looking out into the few folks gathered in the end zone that were watching our practice. "*** damn son who are you? We need you for the season," one old man said. I turned around to jog back and there was the corner who was guarding me all up in my face. "You think you gone embarrass me huh?" I grabbed his facemask with both of my hands and flung him to the turf. The team quickly got between us both and broke it up, but not before I embarrassed him again with shoving his head into the ground two to three times. I talked mess all the way back to the huddle, catching eye contact with coach on my way back. He smiled and gave me a wink.

"ALRIGHT D!!! WHAT THE HELL WAS THAT!!!"

He was now lighting into their ass, but he knew what was up. He knew the power of underestimation and they had truly underestimated me. As I prepared for the next play, coach pulled me out. "Mark, your in. Son, if you can do that for me all year long, you won't have to worry about that GI Bill paying for school. This school will pay for you to play here." He patted me on the shoulder and went back to coaching his defense. He called me in for a few more plays and the results were much of the same. Two touchdowns on the number one defense and a bunch of passes caught over the middle for some great yardage. As practice winded down, Lance came over to me. "You in there man. I ain't never seen a first day impact like that in my life. And you slaughtered Killa Cam on the first play from scrimmage. It ain't too many on the team, let alone the conference who can say they did that. Now just imagine if you were out here last year with us?" I wasn't so much worried about making the team. I was more concerned about making an impact. The season came with the quickness. I wore that number 12 jersey with pride. Eleven made up the number of players on both sides of the ball. I wanted to be 12. The unknown factor. The one that everyone looked down on and didn't pay attention too. Through the first six games, I didn't do much. I mean, I made some key catches, but Lance and the twins took the bulk of the yards. I simply had 18 catches for 246 yards, which came out to be something like 13 yards a catch. Then came the game against Northern Colorado. We were down there visiting in the thin air of Greeley in non-conference action. They may have been Division II, but they were not too far removed from back to back national titles, so we weren't taking them lightly. Austin went down the previous game with a torn ACL and was out for the season. That's when coach threw me in. We were 5-1 and undefeated in conference play. I don't know if Jesus was in the cheering section that day, but he had to be there in some shape, form or fashion. Right out the gate, Max, our QB, linked up with me for an 85-yard bomb for a touchdown. This non-factor had finally did something. Then, it only got better from there. It seemed like their secondary was on vacation and the D line was packing up to catch the next flight. Ball after ball came my way. I ran so much that game that you would've thought that the police were chasing me. In the end, we romped those suckers in their own backyard 73-3. Eight catches, 287 yards receiving, with five touchdowns. 85, 56, 24, 39 and 52. That was 256 on just five catches alone. My life was made after that day and I was no longer the unknown. The world now knew. As we were on the flight home, the television on the plane was locked on Sportscenter. "Top ten play #1 comes out of Northern Colorado tonight where Darnell P. King. **DPK!!! BOOYAH!!!** Hit 'em with the okey doke son. Eight catches, 287 yards and five, count 'em, **FIVE** touchdowns from 85, 56, 24, 39 and 52 yards out. I don't know the kid, but he's JJ from Good Times. Dy-no-mite." The plane erupted in love as Lance crazy ass rubbed my head and the rest of the folks in my seat vicinity did the same. They were happy that someone from the squad made it to ESPN. I was simply happy that my highlights were narrated by Stuart Scott. Who in the hell wouldn't want their highlights narrated by the innovator of hip hop in sports broadcasting? When I stepped foot back onto campus, a new star was born. I refocused on everything from school, to community service, to the football field. I was just a sophomore living a big-time dream. Much of the same occurred as I entered my junior year. But, again, we fell short come playoff time. Another final four appearance, but yet no advancement to the title game. That year I made first team all-conference, as I finished with 79 catches for 1,392 yards and 14 touchdowns. Then, came my senior year. I was high on everyone's draft boards. Lance was gone and graduated, so I was the focus of everything. It was championship or die. That's the mindset that I had set in my head. You can't become a millionaire with a thousand-dollar mindset. Nor could you become a winner with a loser's mindset. You show me a joyful and happy loser, and I will simply show you a loser. We were 12-3 going into the national title game. There waiting for us were the Black Bears of Maine. They had never been here, nor had even scratched the surface of a national title game before. They were the darlings of this year. They wanted to shock the world, but we wanted to blow up the planet. There we were, down 27-23 in the waning time of the fourth. 14 seconds to be exact. Fourth and goal at our own 3-yard line. It was now or never. As we broke the huddle, I knew the ball was coming to me. I was gonna motion in towards the tight end, break across the back of the end zone, behind the linebackers and be left wide open. Just as planned, I motioned in right off the ass of my tight end. The ball was snapped. The linebackers were confused as two of us were coming the same way. The fake pitch sold it perfectly as I saw free reign. Our QB threw the ball. No one was around me as I hit the back of the end zone. In full celebration mode, I reached out for the pass. It was a little high so I had to jump to catch it. Caught. I immediately threw the ball into the stands and dropped to my knees in the end zone. Hard work had finally paid off. However, amidst the roar of the crowd, there was no signal for a touchdown. I got up, looking at the refs along with players from both sides. They kept us away as they continued to discuss. It was a full-fledged catch, so I didn't know what in the good hell they could be discussing. Suddenly, the head official with the white hat signaled with both arms that I was out of bounds. I heard the Maine fans erupting, while I knew our fans were in stunned silence. I looked up at the giant screen on the scoreboard. My left foot had come down where the chalk and the green of the end zone met. From what we all saw, there was a slight amount of green between the back end and my foot. From another angle, not so much. I couldn't argue it or dispute it, nor coach. Replays had to be conclusive and this certainly wasn't. I just fell to the ground in that moment. My teammates tried to pick me up off the field, but it was to no avail. I wasn't getting up. Finally, I literally had to be carried to the bench. No one was speaking to me and for good reason. I sat on the end of the bench and just bawled my eyes out.

Dr. Pizar just stared at me, twirling his pen around. "You know I was there at that game Darnell. I knew who you were the second you walked in. I didn't wanna tell myself that this was the kid who questionably didn't get in bounds and would've given my alma mater a national title. Nor did I wanna tell myself that this is the person who beat up a young Grizzly who got out of hand. Nor did I wanna tell myself that this was the kid who didn't punch the quarterback for throwing such an inaccurate ball. I know what it's like to be at the bottom. I started from the bottom. But I need your word. If I give you this job, you teach these kids what the real meaning of suffering is. I don't need someone who will just get them physically strong. I need someone who can strengthen their minds. See the brain is a marvelous creature. In a split second it can tell you something is hot and cause a reaction. It can signal you to do amazing things. I don't care about your felony. I don't care about a bullshit no touchdown call. I need a man who will help make these boys men. Now, are you up for the challenge? Coach?" He smiled at me. I didn't wanna get to ecstatic, but with a gracious smile back, I told him, "Yes sir."

"You start Monday he told me. I don't think you have to worry about scraping pennies as a mechanic anymore." I looked at him oddly.

"How'd you know I worked as a mechanic?"

"I was running your file on my computer here while you told me your story. I got ways to find out information. Trust, it's all a part of the process. But again, you're going to be paid good, so I expect you to be tough on these kids."

"Sir, every Tuesday I have a meeting with ex-felons in the evenings, followed by a counseling session with a young kid who is in there with me."

"I'll tell you what then. Tuesday, you are off, but I offer you another challenge. You get that kid to come here so we can correct him. I don't care about skin color, attitude, any of that. You can fix anything that is broken. Let's get this young man an education. I deal with all of these black athletes that come up too little white North Dakota. Now, I don't say that in a demeaning way. But, we know that these kids are out of their element up here. Hell, in a lot of places, most don't even care about them. Just use them up for some games, make billions and that's it. They give them the boot out the door with a piece of paper. That shit isn't fair at all. Now me, and this is just me. I sign a secret pact with all of my black football players up here. It's individual and under the table. I break them off with $1000 after each game."

"Out of your own pocket?," I interrupted.

"No. Boosters. So, you figure 10-15 games a year. That's ten to fifteen thousand that those kids see. It's still chump change compared to what these schools make, but I couldn't sleep at night knowing that these kids are busting their ass and aren't getting something in return."

"Sounds like you grew up around black folks' sir."

"Naw. I'm from here. But my wife. Oh yeah. My wife is black. I can never understand what a black individual goes through because I'm not one. However, what I can try to do is empathize and play my part."

"Do you look out for the white kids?" He folded his hands and looked me square in the eye. "Darnell, let me explain something that you may already know. When you're white, you are born with an advantage and a privilege. Money or no money, they are gonna have it regardless. Most white people may not wanna admit that, but it's the truth. My kids. My biracial kids, I already know they will get hell in life. I got married knowing what I was getting into and what they were gonna face. But we can finish talking about this later. Back to the kid under your wing. It's only fair that he gets the same shot as they do, even if he can't dribble a basketball or throw a football. Now, let's do great things." We shook hands, I exited his office and headed out of the building. Once I got to the car,

I immediately began to cry and praise God. After a long time of struggling, he had finally put me in a position to where I could start to achieve great things in life again. Life was sometimes cold, but it was fair, just like the pimp game.

TRUTH SESSION #2

NO MATTER WHAT direction I looked in, I saw nothing but iron bars. Yoked up young men who were savages in their own right. Being stuck here could either make or break you. For me, it had been years since I had become a part of this lifestyle. Every day, you found yourself nearing the breaking point. I had become so used to it. I was damn near immune to the sounds of iron bars clanking together. The screams of 1,000 other men, as with each scream, they released a small bit of frustration. The smell of tension was in the air at all times. Once again, another day was about to end, and I was simply just another number in this everlasting lifestyle. Only now, I wasn't identified by a five-digit prison number. **"LIFT THAT SHIT COREY!!!"** I held my hands underneath the bar as Corey pressed up rep number eight of 315 pounds. **"TWO MO' SON!!! TWO MO'!!!"** By the time I finished screaming that, he had pressed up for nine, but I could tell that his arms were damn near to the point of death. He got the bar down to his chest for his last rep. **"UGHHH!!!,"** he yelled out, as this was the struggle of struggles trying to get this up. **"I AIN'T HELP-**

ING!!! I AIN'T HELPING!!!," I repeatedly screamed at him. With all that the kid had left in him, somehow, he managed to get it up to rack it. **"WOOOO!!! THAT'S THE SHIT I'M TALKING BOUT MAN!!! MUTHAFUCKIN BEAST!!!"** He just lay there exhausted. "Now, this is what you have to do. Exert that strength. I can't bear to see anyone ever bully you in the post like they did in that tournament game. Understand me?"

"Yes sir," he replied. After that full workout, we had finished off with a marathon rep from one to ten, with 185 pounds on the bar. Now, you may think that's nothing to a kid who had just pressed 315 ten times. However, at this point, his arms were like noodles. This is just how things went down over here at the farm, the nickname that the university gym had. It was a far cry from prison, but I tried to make the workouts as brutal as I had experienced in my day. The great CT Fletcher had once said that *"I command you to grow."* I wanted these boys here to grow mentally and physically with no limitations. "Good shit my man. Now, you know next time it's gonna be even more grueling, but I want you to take it in stride. Understand me?"

"Yes sir" he replied, breathing heavy with sweat pouring down his forehead. We dapped up and put an X across our chest before he headed out. I swear Black Panther had started something. Brothers were putting X's across their chest after dappin up. People were hollin out Wakanda forever at the most random times. It was definitely funny, but amazing at the same time. I now had time for myself, as most of the guys from the basketball team were done with their session. I stepped outside the gym to an area they called "*The Pit.*" Eight sets of grueling tire flips commenced. I felt like a new individual now that I was back to strength training on a regular. One thing these kids had taught me was how to push my own self. I was accepted with open arms, and I for one was happy that the students loved my style. It was early afternoon on this Tuesday. May showers were not in effect at all. I loved my schedule. Working early mornings and being off when the afternoon was still early gave me all the time in the world. It kept me busy and prevented me from just sitting at home, doing absolutely nothing. As I headed home for the day, I thought about how blessed I was again. Then, I started to think about the talk me and Dr. Pizar had. Get Twon in here so he could start on his path to become a better individual. Not just for himself, but for the community alike. More importantly, I wanted to do the right thing and bring him over to the side away from all the bullshit. Life has some old, sneaky tricks I tell you. No one ever said that people would always do right. People were manipulative, much like I was back in my day. I could make something good into evil and vice versa. I had a mission. A soul to save. Tonight, that mission would continue with the meeting, followed by our time at the dinner table. I got home that early afternoon a little bit after 12 and got some much-needed downtime, meaning a nap. Training young men took the life out of you. At around three, I woke up to the sound of someone beating on my door. I don't even remember falling asleep on the couch while watching Martin, but obviously I did. Here we go again, I thought. Twon's mom was probably back to Pulp Fiction my black ass. **"FUCK!!!,"** I yelled, as I stubbed my pinky toe on the edge of the couch. How the hell I didn't avoid a whole couch beat the hell outta me. I guess I was still tired. I hobbled over to the front door, still speaking in tongues on how great God was or wasn't. I opened it up to see Twon standing there. "What you doing here young buck? We don't meet up until after the meeting."

"My moms kicked me out OG." I stood there in disbelief trying to comprehend what he had just told me. "You wanna run that by me one more time?"

"She kicked me out OG. I have no place to go. I'm homeless. All I have is the clothes on my back. Please, please, can I crash here until I get on my feet?" I looked both ways out the door, readjusting my eyes to the light. "Come in here and sit down," I told him. He came in with the quickness, sitting down and shivering on the couch. All I could do was shake my head. "You shivering in the month of May bruh. I know you ain't cold, so just calm down man. You're okay."

"Okay OG. Just give me a minute." I walked over to the kitchen to boil a pot of water, still looking at him as he rocked back and forth in a hurt mindset. I had to make me some hot chocolate, chill it in the fridge and gulp it down. Don't judge me. "You know I got one question about something you said when you came through that door. How are you gonna stay here until you get on your feet, when you ain't never stood on your own two before?"

"Huh," as he looked up at me. "Exactly what I said young man. How are you gonna stay here without the ability to contribute? You ain't never stood on your own two, so how can I wait for you to get on your feet?" He was dead silent.

I had taken the soul right out of his body. "I'll tell you what. We make a deal. You get your GED, or get a job, and I will get you in college, or on your feet."

"I thought we already had a deal. And, how you gone get me in something that you don't even have access to OG?" I walked over to the kitchen table, grabbing and tossing over my staff badge to him. His eyes got big. He couldn't believe what he was seeing. "Yo. When you get this?"

"That's not the point. Just know I got hired on as a strength coach for the university. Trust me, I got access. But you ain't having no access to anything unless you agree to terms here. See, my house. My rules. Also, you'll be in here every night by 9 p.m. No friends or strangers will be brought up in here. Every night, we gone go over your schooling stuff or whatever. Deal?" He stood up off the couch waving his hands back and forth. "Naw OG. I'm a grown man. If I'm staying here, you gone treat me as such."

"I am treating you as such. I'm giving you a chance to make a grown man decision. Now either you can accept it, or you can roam the streets of Fargo tonight. And it's lonely as ever on those streets. It may not be cold as polar bear nuts out there, but it's still hard on the streets when you ain't got nowhere to go. I know you ain't bout that life. And I know you don't want that. Its penguins that would rather chill in Antarctica than be up here in Fargo. So, it's your choice." I went back to the kitchen to pour up my hot chocolate. "Deal," he said. "But what do you have to do?"

"Me," as I chuckled at the question and put the cup in the fridge. "I just gotta keep working and paying the bills. That's what me has to do. See one thing you gotta realize is this. Even though I made mistakes in the past, I've been your age. You ain't been mine. I was in college at 18, so I think I have a good clue of what I'm doing here in this situation. Now, tomorrow, we gone hit the store to get you some new clothes, shoes, all that. Soon, I'll be moving up out of here and into something that I should've had my whole adult life. Until then, you gone get man training one on one."

"Yo, if you talkin' about going to Ross or Burlington, or something of that nature, naw. I can't do it. I can't be wearing no cheap clothes."

"Also, you'll attend service with me and some of the ex-felons every Sunday. No service, or, no service here."

"Do I really have a choice?," he asked. "As a matter of fact, you do. It's part of the process of being a grown man. See I don't operate on do I really have a choice. You always have a choice. Same way I had a choice to walk away when that kid spit in my face, but I didn't. Same way I had a choice when I could've given up and robbed people. Same way I had a choice to not to go search for a job, and just wait until something better came along. Now, what you have to realize is that choice is something no one can ever take from you. You gotta choice Monday through Friday to go to those GED classes. You don't have to show up. Even if you don't, the instructor still gets paid. They still go home at night and sleep in a comfortable bed."

"SO, WHAT ABOUT THE CHOICE I DIDN'T HAVE TO COME TO FUCKING NORTH DAKOTA!!!" I had to pause because the elder in me wanted to choke this kid because

I didn't know who the hell he thought he was raising his voice at. A quick prayer got echoed in my head and I stayed calm. "First off youngin," as I stuck my right arm out, palm down. "Tone that shit down," as I lowered my arm slowly. "You may be from a big city, but you don't want these problems. You right. You didn't have a choice because your mama was in charge. But, you did have a choice to adapt and overcome when you got here. Did you? No. And look where it has gotten you. Now, two things we need to get clear. One, you will never raise your voice at me when I never raised my voice at you. Two, you will never raise your voice at me because I just may lose my religion and beat yo ass. B, son or whatever y'all say in New York. Now, you be ready by 4:27, because I'm leaving out the door at 4:30 sharp for our meeting." I walked off and headed into the bathroom to take a shower. What he was doing out there, I had no clue and really didn't care. I believed, however, that I had gotten through to the kid.

———————

"Well, well, well. What you dummies been up to since the last time we left?" It seemed no one wanted to answer Cleavon, as his bright red gators may have been distracting everyone. Or, it may have been the rainbow-colored socks. I didn't know what it was with these Midwest cats. They'll wear a pink suit and call it pepto bismol. That's just how they were. "Well," I said, trying not to laugh at those God-awful socks. "I found an occupation through the grace of God that has me on the right track back in life. I'm one of the new strength coaches over at the university." The room was overjoyed as my fellow ex con buddies applauded and patted me on the back. "Also, I have a new roommate."

"What's her name?," Cleavon said. We all started laughing. "Naw. His name is Twon." Everyone got silent and looked at him, including me. "Umm Darnell?"

"**HELL NAW CLEAVON!!!**," I yelled at him. "It ain't shit like that. I ain't with the wishy-washy stuff. Naw. I took him in. His mother kicked him out. Why? I dunno. I just know he needed a place, so I made my home his home." Twon's head was down in despair. "Oh ok. Cause for a minute I thought you had a flashback of prison," Cleavon said. "Man please. I ain't get raped once in the joint."

"But I know you had to fight for your asshole at least once or twice in there."

"Yeah, and those muthafuckas never got it."

"Aight, aight. Calm down. I did 17 and a lot of it was in solitary for whooping ass. Now. Antwon. You wanna tell us what happened to get you kicked out of your mama's pad?"

"No, but do I really have a choice?"

"Yeah you little peghead muthafucka you do." Twon looked at Cleavon, possibly trying to intimidate him with a mean mug. However, that shit wasn't gone work. I leaned over to Twon and whispered to him. "You better be careful with that shit. Don't let that old age fool you. He will fuck you up. And, he stay strapped." I told that to him and went back to sitting straight. He looked over at me, then back at Cleavon. Cleavon was just sitting there, glasses down off his eyes, head tilted down, waiting for the young brother's response. "So, Monday night, my mom was still at work. She wasn't coming home until about ten. I finished up my GED class around seven and another girl in my class came home with me. We sat in the house drinking and shit. Then, things started to get a little wild. Sniff this line with me, she asked. I had never seen cocaine before. Like, I seen it on TV and shit, but never in front of me like that. I figured what the hell. It can't do that much damage to me. We ended up sniffing two lines each. We lost track of time and really our minds as a whole. Long story short, when my mama came in, we were in her bedroom. I was sitting in a chair and shorty head was between my legs. Moms came in the bedroom and absolutely flipped. She didn't touch ol' girl, as at this point she was running for her life. She came right after me and slapped the dog pis out of me. All I know next was that she was yelling she was tired and she was through, and not in those words. She told me to get out and live on the streets since I didn't wanna respect her house anymore. Last night, I slept under a bridge, with a dusty old blanket that she threw at me on the way out. It was the most painful feeling ever. This morning, I found myself begging for loose change near 7 Eleven. It hurt my pride. I eventually mustered up enough dough to get a sandwich. Then, I thought about OG and wandered over to his house, asking him can I stay with him. That's it." The room was dead silent. It seemed Cleavon was in his pimp thinking process. The wild colors of his socks seemed to change colors. "Alright. What we seem to have here is a failure to communicate. So, let me do this. Fellas, how many of you have been kicked out of anything due to you not wanting to follow the rules?" The whole room raised their hands in unison. "See here Twon. You gotta realize one thing young buck. All of us are rehabilitated men. Some of us may look older than what we are, but it's a reminder of what once was. We ain't that no more. Look at Kelvin. Years of drug abuse makes him shake. His mama, still right here. Is he doing better? Yes, he is. Even with the effects of years of abusing dope, he still doing better. We've been there. Right now, you think ya shit don't stink, and ya think cause ya dick touch the toilet water when you sit down that you are a man. Naw. A man ain't made by his dick. A man is made with his mind. Now, I see someone who probably had the best news in the eight years I been doing this. A strength coach. At a good university. His pay scale just went from mechanic to self-sufficient. He ain't gotta scramble together pennies all night. He gone eat, shit and sleep well. And now, he's giving you the chance to do the same. So, I'm telling you right now Twon. Don't blow this. We are here and we love you. You already headed in the right direction with ya GED courses, but you can't mess this up. Remember. I don't care if the whole world helps you. Every man is responsible for his own destiny. You got all these black folks who have a knack to say so and so set us back. Naw. You set yourself back. If you're putting yourself in the same category as another individual who don't know you from the man on the moon, then what you are telling yourself is that you are failing because of someone else's actions. It doesn't work like that youngster. Never has. Never will. Only fools blame others." I took in more of what he said than probably anyone in the room. We continued on that night for another hour and some change. We were supposed to be out of here by six, but Cleavon was on one tonight. I admired dude. An ex-pimp out of Chicago. Nickname on the streets used to be VLAD. Her wore a lot of plaid suits and replaced the P with VL, his reference to his days as a Vice Lord on the West Side of the city. He had pimped for a good few years strong, until one fateful night. He said he was exiting his red, black and gold lac when he was ambushed. He was shot 12 times. The shooters took off, but amazingly, Cleavon was able to drive himself to the hospital just some blocks away. He went through eight months of agonizing surgeries and rehabilitation. Once over, he gave the lifestyle up, but only for a short period of time. He got back in the game, but this time, he upped the ante. Drugs got added to the mix. In the blink of an eye it seemed, he got caught up. A 17-year bid was handed down to him in the Illinois Department of Corrections. Once out in '99, he came to North Dakota, left his kids there with his baby mamas' and started a new. He got into mentorship heavy and that was all she wrote. Since those days, he has rekindled the relationship with his kids. Two of them moved up here and he is now a grandfather. So, my man's knows all about struggle and pain. "So, what you think about tonight?," I asked Twon as we got in the car. "I mean. It was eye opening. I'm just hoping I find my way in the world."

"You will young brother. You will," I told him. "C'mon. Let's head to Ross really quick and pick you up some stuff." We got to Ross on this crispy spring night and I could tell he was a little bit uncomfortable. "Look, I'll never buy something out of here."

"Ain't nothing to be ashamed of shopping in here. All these folks in here for a reason. Cause it's good shopping." We walked in and headed right for the clothing section. "I see you ain't nothing more than 5'9. Probably about a 32 in the waist I assume."

"34 OG."

"Okay Cool. Get you five or six pairs of jeans, and then we'll look at the shoes. Get some joints that look good. Don't be searching for no old Girbaud jeans. Cash Money took over for the nine-nine and the 2000. Not the one seven and the 2018. Matter fact. Here. Lemme see something." I pulled out a tape measure. "Yo whatcha doing OG?," as Twon jumped back. "Trust me man. Ain't no one reaching for ya nuts. Just trying to measure you."

"Man make this quick man. I ain't trying to have these folks think I'm sweet boy Lou over here."

"Man shut up," as I raised up. "Stretch your arms out to your sides." He obliged and I measured him around his chest and down his arms. "Aight man. Got it."

"What was that for?"

"You just getting normal clothes right now. One day, you gone have to get in a suit."

"Naw, that ain't me OG." I shook my head and let him be as he moved it over to the shoe section. I was watching him. Not to see if he would steal, because I know he wasn't gone try that in here. I just wanted to see how he accepted this new chapter of his life. As I found me my own pair of Nike's to take home, here he came, with six shirts to match his jeans. "Is this cool OG?" I looked through the clothes. To my surprise, he got all collared shirts. "Impressive. You start becoming a man when you start looking like one. And you can definitely look like one with these fits. Now, pick out one of these all white pairs of shoes and let's roll. What's your size?"

"12"

"Boy I wish I had some small feet like you. It's damn near an adventure trying to find size 15's anywhere on this earth."

"Damn OG. A 15? You wearing the whole shoebox huh?" He laughed, but I didn't find shit funny. He got his shoes and we headed for the register. It all came out to $100 even. I hadn't seen my first check from the university, but I did have a stash of cash that I used for rainy days. Today was one of those stormy ones. We made it back to the house at around eight. "We having Swedish meatballs in gravy tonight. Stove Top is the big homey tonight. You good with that?"

"Yeah," he replied. I cut the oven on and threw the entrée in there on a baking sheet, for the quick 15-20 minute warm up. "Come on over here man. You know our routine."

"Man, you got a new job and you still got this table?"

"Why not? Does this table not serve a purpose like your life?" He was quiet as a mouse. "Now sit down." He sat down at the table as I grabbed myself an A&W. I needed to stop drinking these things. I knew it was death and diabetes in a can, but I was hooked on these things. "So. Gimme the rundown. Was that head worth it?"

"Worth what?"

"Worth getting kicked out of the house for. I mean, you gotta look at life like this Twon. Yeah, I have my days where I get upset that I ain't where I wanna be. Yeah, I have my days where I am happy where I am. But one thing remains. I'll never do anything to jeopardize what I have. Now, you're probably thinking well what about your fight. Correct, I could've handled it a different way, but I didn't. I don't know any adult that would. But, you deliberately disrespected that woman's house. You put your body at even more risk sniffing lines. Do you know what coke does to you? As a matter of fact, I'm pouring this pop out right now and declaring that I ain't drinking 'em no more because it's killing me. That powder is like this pop. Oh yeah. It looks good, feel good, maybe even taste good. But, what are the long-term effects? How is your mind gonna receive it? I tell you, it won't be a pleasant feeling. Now in the living room you got a big bag of clothes. Most of them are button ups. Why?"

"Well, honestly OG. I just figured that you weren't gonna let me buy any t-shirts or anything like that, since that ain't being a grown man in your eyes."

"Go grab one of those shirts and put it on," I told him. He got up and went over to the bag, sorting through it until he found the red and grey one. "Put it on." Once he did, I saw him literally drown in that shirt. "What size is that man?"

"3X."

"**3X!!!** You know how tacky you look right now? You look like you in a pair of navy steamers or something."

"Well you wanted me to look like a grown man, right?"

"A grown man would've made the decision to go to the fitting room and ensure it was the proper size. That shit is a nightgown. Now take out the pairs of jeans you bought." He went back to the bag and pulled out all the jeans. "Aww man," he said.

"Sup?"

"I picked out two pairs of skinnies. I didn't mean too, but I don't wear skinnies."

"Well you better find some use for 'em, cause I ain't just about to waste my money on something and you not gonna use it."

"C'mon OG."

"C'MON MY ASS!!! Man up." I knew he wasn't feeling what I was saying, but I had to teach him the consequences of making choices and failing to make conducive ones. After a good 20 minutes, the food was ready and we sat at the table as usual. I pulled out the plates and spilt the family sized meal in half. "Pray," I told him. "You know I don't believe in God."

"I know you don't. That's why I said pray." We stared at each other for quite a while with neither one of us budging. "You ain't eating until we pray."

"Father."

"Hold up. Join hands."

"OG you said pray. Not go on a date."

"Just join hands. Now close your eyes and pray."

"Father, thank you for this food and a place to stay. Amen."

"So, why'd you say Father if you don't believe in God?"

"I dunno. I always heard my mother say it so I figured that's how I say it."

"You do believe then. Cause if you didn't, you wouldn't have said Father. See you gotta belief, but you so stuck on what's been going wrong in your life that you tell yourself there is no God because nothing goes well for you. And that right there is the worst kind of mental to have. If you noticed, I ain't cursed in front of you not one time right now. Yeah, I know I've let off on you in the past. Hell, not even five minutes ago. I got that. But, now, I'm trying to watch what rolls off my tongue. The power of life and death is in the tongue. As quick as I can speak life into you, I can also speak death into you. See I learned a long time ago that my words are powerful. Man, when I used to speak in college, the whole room snapped to attention like I was a military general. Whether it was spoken word or just a class presentation, I had 'em locked in."

"Wait a minute, wait a minute OG. You used to do spoken word?"

"I dabbled in it back in my heyday. It's a gift that I possess. Why? You do spoken word?"

"I mean. I like poetry. Like writing thoughts to free your mind helps me get through days that I don't wanna be here." I took a huge gulp of them Swedish meatballs and gravy. "Spit something for me?"

"What?," Twon said, with pasta hanging out of his mouth.

"Spit something for me. Freestyle poetry off the top of your dome?"

"I can't man. I ain't that good."

"Just try. You'd be amazed at what you can do once you try."

"Alright, here goes nothing."

"*Spending time in a mother's womb, feeling like a king trapped in an Egyptian tomb, lost knowledge and riches yet to be discovered, much like the thought process of an uneducated brother, you see, when they call me dumb founded, its cause that's the foundation of my membrane, not fully developed yet*

70

*thirsting for knowledge, that's why I take showers to try and quench the power of...*Damn OG. I can't do it anymore."

"**THAT WAS GOOD MAN!!! WHAT YOU MEAN YOU CAN'T DO IT!!! THERE'S YOUR GIFT!!!**" He cracked a smile at me as we continued eating. "You see all it takes is stepping out on faith. You said you couldn't do it, but you did it. Now, you just have to manifest that gift into something powerful so that others can be impacted by it. It's pointless to have something and not share it with the world. All it takes is a little bit of faith and magic."

"So how you know God is real OG?"

"I know cause I'm here and not in a casket. Not still locked down behind the walls with people telling me when and where to eat. When and where to go to sleep at. I'm here and not in a negative place in my life anymore. That's how I know it's real. I ain't trying to make you into an all-star Christian where you slam dunking the Bible all over people's heads. Nah, that ain't my job. My job, as a God-fearing man is to open you up to the love He has for us, so that you can spread that love one day. Trust, the same way that I am helping you now, you will one day be in my shoes helping someone else. By that time, I may be long gone from this earth. Heck, I may still be here. Either way, my job is to see you get better and reach the level of manhood that I know you are capable of. The first step, though, the first step, is that you have to leave everything in the past and not be afraid to begin anew." He shook his head and I shook mines back. We finished off dinner that night and he begin to delve in his books for GED classes. Somewhere during the middle of the night, around 1 a.m., I peered out of my bedroom and looked at him sleep. He was sleeping with such peace now. I smiled because I felt this kid had finally started to believe in himself. I noticed the outfit he had laid out on the ironing board. It wasn't ironed, but the fact he took the time to pick out what he was gonna wear later today showed me a lot about his plans for the future. As I was heading back toward my bed, I saw that my phone had started to buzz. I checked the text message that flashed across the screen. *"You killing him with the Jesus shit ain't you?"* I shook my head and just closed my phone. The next morning, we got up and I dropped him off at the center for his daily studies. I headed on to campus at about 7:30. "Hey Darnell. You hear ya man Corey pounded the boards last night?"

"Naw, I didn't. What he look like? Better yet. Where the hell is he playing cause the season over with?"

"Undisciplined and out of control," Doc told me. Doc was one of the assistant coaches of the basketball team. "He seemed like he harnessed his energy in the right way, but his output wasn't up to par."

"Okay, but where was he playing at?"

"Little something I organized with a local semi pro team." Just as he said that, Corey and other members of the team walked through the door. **"COREY!!!,"** I yelled out. "What's up coach?," as he jogged over. "Holla at me in the office real fast." I walked in and took a seat at my desk trying to figure out what was wrong with this kid. "Coach is that you?," as he pointed to the pic on my desk. "Yep. That's me. Grizzly for life. Three of the best years of my life."

"I ain't know you did your thang on the field. Did y'all ever take the whole ship?" I paused, twirling my pen in my hand. I could assume that the kid was being funny, but it was obvious that he didn't know anything. "Nope. Not at all son. I dropped the game winning pass on fourth down in the fourth quarter of the championship game my senior year."

"Aww coach, man I ain't mean to bring up that."

"It's cool man. It's cool. So how did you do last night? I heard not to good." He slouched in his chair and took a deep breath. "Man coach. I was trying to remember everything you said about not being bullied. So, I don't know if coach told you, but he organized this game against a semi pro team. We knew it was illegal, but that ain't the point. I started off well, but then he got to talking. I lost my cool. One foul led to the next. I just didn't have my mind right."

"How many rebounds you have?"

"I scored 19 you know."

"I don't need to know how many points you scored. How many rebounds did you have?" "Three," he answered, with a dead look in his eyes.

"Three rebounds. After all the lifting and advice, you got three funky rebounds. Now, what does that tell me? It tells me that you taking the advice I gave you all wrong. See, the game of basketball, rather sports ain't about being the flashiest guy out there who can score the most points. Now, I already know how you did before I brought you in here. You fouled out. You were so concerned about being a beast that you turned into a beauty. A drama queen. You let someone get in your head, throw you off of your game and the strength you channeled was one to bully. You gotta play smart. 99% of the game is using your head. You ever see Dennis Rodman, Charles Oakley or Xavier McDaniel care about scoring 25-30 a game? No, you didn't. They did the dirty work. Without the dirty work, you won't win. Point blank period. I'm not telling you this for my health. I'm telling you this because it's true."

"I know coach, I know. I just didn't want that game to be the last game I remembered. I didn't wanna get bullied and just embarrass myself." That's when I hit him with it. "You only embarrass yourself when you don't do your job. No man can look down on another man for an honest effort. But he can look down on a man when he tries to do something that he is not capable of. See you can do anything, but you can't do everything. Now let's get out in this gym and work some more."

"Aight coach."

"Gimme five minutes. I'll be out there." Corey left the office and I just rubbed my face. All the shit I just told him, and I couldn't even be honest with him about how I actually lost the game. I needed to listen to my own damn self. As I headed out, even more life lessons started to flash back in my cranial, because sometimes, sports related to life in ways that we could never imagine.

———————————

It was 2004 when I attempted to start a new life. I was two years removed from college and the gig I had was a well-paying one. Six figures out of school was a blessing indeed, but it didn't allow me the free time that I wanted in life. The 9 to 5 took eight hours of my life every day, and I knew that I was talented enough to have all 24 to do what I wanted to do. I sat in a room full of unknowns about to listen to someone else who was completely unknown to me. A friend had invited me out to a conference here in Portland, Oregon, where I moved to about a year after I had graduated. Some company had taken the internet and marketing world by storm. Now, I wasn't the one for overnight, get rich quick schemes, but I decided to take a listen just to quell my own curiosity. "I'm telling you Darnell. If you invest in this now and spread it vividly, I promise you that we both can take the world by storm?"

"We?," I asked Tom. "We or me?"

"You know what I mean brother?" Funny thing about some people was that they automatically thought your benefit would be their benefit. It's like some cats that make the NBA. They'll go home and people just be begging for money. Then, if they don't give 'em none, all of a sudden they try and hit them with a guilt trip story. Man, I gave you your first basketball. Man, I was the one on the sidelines with the gun when you were playing cross town just to make sure those other niggas didn't trip on you. People had this knack to make you feel low as an excuse for their laziness in life. I mean hell, I'm pretty sure I could rescue a snake out of a wire fence, but it doesn't mean I'm supposed to get mad if he don't come back and eat all the gophers around my house. I just laughed at it all in the back of my mind. "Welcome all. Welcome." The crowd erupted in an astounding roar for this brother who came out on stage and hadn't even said his name yet. Tom was next

75

to me on his feet, looking like a seventh-grade school girl who had met the young Justin Bieber. Me, I wanted to see numbers. Kiss my ass for the standing ovation shit. "My name is Julian. Let me welcome you to the first day of the rest of your lives." It was an impressive first statement I will say that. It still didn't woo me over. As the presentation moved along, the numbers looked very impressive for this company. I had never heard of them a day in my life. But, then again, it's a lot of things I hadn't heard of in my life. I sat here for the next hour or so listening to stories from random people on how this company changed their lives financially. That's cool and all, but what did it do for them personally outside of the money? That was my biggest question. I wasn't so much concerned about money, because that comes and goes. Numbers never end and if you put all of your power into numbers, you will never be happy in life. I was already situated in this world. I had a great niche as a personal trainer with a sort of side slash full time gig as a freelance writer. Financial freedom was a pretty penny living in this world, so what more could they offer me was my biggest question. "Darnell, this is the man I want you to meet. His name is Julian. One of the top reps in this company."

"Sup brother."

"Nothing much man."

"So, Tom tells me you're interested in the business." I looked at Tom with that side eye look, knowing damn well he lied, but it was whatever. "Naw bruh, I just honestly came to see what y'all were about. It's not my thing."

"What's not your thing? Making money?"

"Naw. I do that brother. Trust me. That's proof by the new Lac truck sitting outside on 24's. Selling things ain't my forte. I write and keep cats physically fit." He laughed at me. "Brother man. Trust, the only thing I am selling is opportunity. Hey, let's be clear though, if you say no, I won't lose any sleep at night. What I am telling you is to not pass up on something great. I love to see brothers in this business doing the damn thing, and I would love for you to join the winning team. Tom's life has already changed. Ask him." I looked at Tom and he was sitting there grinning that famous white people's grin. "I'll tell you what brother," I said to Julian. "Let's do an even exchange of services. You come down to my office next week for an interview with the magazine and I'll let you sell me more of what you are trying to get me to buy into." He looked at me crazy. "Brother. That ain't an even exchange. That's just a prop for me. I'm tryna help both of us. Feel me?"

"That's how you see it. The way I see it is this. The magazine is based around fashion and entertainment. Strictly business is something people don't expect from us. Not a lot of people know about the business you are in. So, you get exposure, I highlight a company, the magazine tries a different route, more clients will wanna come to me, more to you and that's that. So, in the end, I'm gonna win for myself regardless. You get your shine. I get my shine. My gift is writing playa. I enhance people. That's what I do. So again, are you coming down, or do I need to find someone else to market?" Things seemed to get tense for a minute. Tom was nervous. I could see it on his face. He probably thought we were about to fight or some mess like that. We were far from that. White people sometimes didn't understand black folks lingo. "Ten Monday morning at your office work for you brother?"

"I'll be there at 9:30."

"That means I'll be there at 9:29." We smiled and shook hands. I liked how my man's operated. We exchanged business cards and he went on about his way. "What the hell was that?," Tom asked me. "That, my friend, is the way you do business. Now, I gotta enjoy the rest of my Saturday."

"Well, thanks for coming out. Hope you two do well."

"Aight Tom." I walked out without a care in the world. Tom was one of those sensitive dudes, so if something didn't go his way, he kind of felt awkward and like he hadn't accomplished anything. It was aight because he was still a good friend and had he not invited me, me and my fellow brother Julian would have never met. I exited the hotel and headed off into the Portland Saturday gloom. The Pacific Northwest was a mutha I tell you when it came to rain. Rain up here was like racism in America. It was simply the norm. I had gotten tired of the hustle and bustle that I called Miami, Florida, where I first moved after graduation. Trust, I missed that place at times. The food, the women, the nightlife. Whatever you wanted, the city of Miami had it. Not to mention, Wade had just joined the Heat when I was down there and was about to take the city and franchise to new heights. I'm not gonna even start on the hip hop and music scene, because that was as diverse and vibrant as ever. Yeah, Miami had it all. I started out there as a master trainer at a gym which frequented the Dolphins, Marlins and every other pro player in the city. When I moved to Portland, I was looking for something different. I always had a knack for writing, and my man's Omarr, who I had crossed paths with on South Beach, offered me six figures to become his beat writer. Now, leaving M-I-Yayo wasn't an easy decision. However, I was young, so I figured why not leave and go to another place for a good while. Something a little bit more chill. I definitely found it in Oregon. Here, things were majorly different. For starters, spotting a brother out here was like spotting Oscar the Grouch in a clean trash can. It was few and far between. A few hood areas were out here, but it damn sure wasn't Dade County. Hell, the Pork-n-Bean Projects alone was tougher than any place out here. That was good for me. I didn't wanna be around wild shootouts and fist fights anymore. I wanted my life to be simple. Next, they had trees. A whole lot of trees. Not palm trees, but actually trees like you see in the forest. It was damn near scary at times how many trees were up here. Green was an understatement. The oxygen was rich and you could breathe. Not like Miami where you were inhaling smoke exhaust down on South Beach from all the cars riding up and down that thang. Lastly, it was the feel of this place. It felt like somewhere you could leave your windows open at night and not have to worry about someone coming in and threatening your livelihood. Now, was I stupid enough to do that in reality? No. But, you get what I'm saying. I rolled downtown to Voodoo doughnuts. This place was legendary, point blank period. To my surprise, the line wasn't a mile long like it usually was. I hurried up and scoured these crazy Portland downtown streets for a parking spot. This place had more one ways and crazy turns than a little bit. I hurried up out the car to get in there before my luck ran out. However, soon as I got in, there was a long line. It just hadn't wound outside yet. It was better than the usual, so I just waited. Now, out here, two donut spots were king. This place and Blue Star. Voodoo had more of a variety when it came to selection. Blue Star simply tasted better, cause their joints were fresh out the grease. I was a sugar junkie and needed to be careful before my black tail caught diabetes. "What's going on Darnell?"

"Nothing much Tunk. Lemme get that joint with the cocoa puffs, Reese's peanut butter cups and all that hot drizzled peanut butter goodness." My mans laughed at how I ordered it. I described it as a woman more than anything. "Aight man. You know the price." I handed him the ten. "You know to keep the change." In Portland, folks took care of each other. It was you scratch my back and I'll scratch yours type of mentality. "There you go man. Til next time."

"Yup. Gotcha," I told Tunk. I came up outta there, sinking my mouth into this sugary goodness. I decided to keep this cool Saturday going and head on down to the Rose Garden where the Trail Blazers played at. This where the new blood Lamarcus Aldridge and crew got it in on a night in and night out basis. Those boys had the tools to win it all, but you know me. I was ride or die Hornets. It was teal and purple til the death of me. That's one thing folks don't understand bout Carolina cats. We were loyal to our soil. It's the Hornets, the Panthers and your choice between the Heels, Dukies, Demon Deacons or Wolf pack. I could care less what anybody gotta say about my state, cause ain't nobody gonna come down there and pop off. We all had a me against the world mentality living out there. All people wanted to know us as was a tobacco state.

In truth, we were a very gritty state with a huge problem called poverty. Charlotte, Fayetteville, Raleigh, they all had major problems that were deep rooted. That was the Carolina that they wanted to keep under wraps. It wasn't good for business. But, it was my business. I wasn't ashamed of home. It's what made me who I was today. I remember watching as a teenager when North Carolina beat Michigan's Fab Five in the national title game. You know, that's the one where C Webb called the infamous "No Timeout." Eric Montross, Ed Davis and crew kept the Tar Heels legacy alive. I remember the party in the city that night they won. Moms had taken me to Charlotte to watch the game. Man, oh man. You talk about a free for all. Anything went that night. It wasn't no black, white, brown, none of that. We were all one school, one unit, one team, one family, one state. That's the beauty of sports. It has the power to bring people together of all backgrounds to celebrate in harmony. It was how I wish life would be on a day in and day out basis. I finished my way through downtown and hopped back on the freeway towards the crib over in Tualatin. I got in that early evening and finished up a few news articles for the magazine. As I was wrapping up the last little bit, Omarr hit me up.

"What's good playa?"

"I got a proposal. What you think about flying to NYC to interview a few bigwigs? It could bank you up to $30,000 playa."

"I'm in bruh. Just let me know when I gotta pack my shit." That was my life when I lived those years in Portland. I had a free moving job, but it took up all of my free time in different aspects. There was no room to settle down, have kids, none of that. I don't regret any of it now. However, I do wish I would've played my cards a little bit differently.

"So how was work today?," Twon asked me, as we kicked back, eating grilled cheese and bacon sandwiches. "It was good. I got my first check. You do the honors." He looked at me kind of weird, but he accepted. He opened it and his eyes got big. **"$5,296 DOLLARS!!!"**

"Schools pay big to keep their athletes in shape young brother. But what you think we should do with the money?"

"I can't tell you that OG. You earned that. I gotta get my own." That's when I leaned in. "What if I told you that if you pass that GED test in two weeks, that this will be your own personal money?" I could see that he still didn't believe me. "Nah OG. You ain't doing that."

"Yes, I will, because you'll be in college. Right there where I work at." He dropped his sandwich in mid bite. "I'm not school material OG. I mean I barely got an 8th grade education."

"But you on the verge of obtaining the equivalent to high school literacy," I told him. "I ain't giving up on you. I told you when we made the deal. I am gonna push you as well as you are gonna push me. I don't back out of my word little bro. At the end of the day, that's all a man has is his word."

"But, what about if I fail?"

"You only fail if you never put forth the effort. Right now, that's the old you talking. You want to not believe in yourself because it's easier. You been doing that your whole life. Not believing in yourself. Start today."

"I'll try, but OG. I don't believe in the devil either man."

"Where did that come from?," I asked him. "I dunno. I was just beating you to the punch before you tried to beat me down with that Jesus stuff."

"Then, what do you believe in Twon?"

"I mean, if you think about it, look at everything from Ancient Egypt. A lot of what the Christian faith uses today came from there. So how am I too believe a book of fables when those same books occurred in someone else's time? Man, they always stealing black folks stuff OG." At that moment, he left me in a stunned silence. You know how sometimes when you wanna say something, but it's best to keep your mouth shut? Well, this was one of those times. As crazy as it may have sounded, the little youngster was right. More importantly, I saw that the boy actually was smart and that he had potential to achieve a lot. "I'm about to call it an early night brother. You clean up here," as I patted him on the back and got up. "You didn't think I knew that huh OG?"

"Knew what?"

"What I just told you. See that's everyone's problem. They think I don't know anything when I actually know a lot. All my life people been treating me like I am some sort of dummy. Like a charity case or some shit. You supposed to be the cat that I am looking up too, yet you just thought the same thing."

"Twon, I never said you were a dummy."

"Yeah, but you never said I was smart either. So why does your God have to be my God?" I already saw where this was going. "Goodnight," as I turned back around and walked towards the bedroom. "Oh, so you walk away from the truth, but you couldn't walk away from the truth a little bit over a year ago." I stopped right before I got to the bedroom. I said a silent prayer in my head because I literally wanted to kill this kid. "Lemme tell you something. I ain't never ran away from nothing in my life. **SO, SHOW SOME FUCKING RESPECT!!!**" Things got real quiet as my eyes were lighting him on fire right now. "I thought you had stop cursing. Devout Christian." My look didn't change, but he was right. He had gotten a reaction out of me that I never saw myself doing at this time in my life. "So why don't you sit down at the dinner table and tell me the story from 2016? Bit by bit. Blow by blow. Help me help you. Right?" He pulled out a chair and went around to the other end of the table to sit down himself. I was still heated and full of rage. Twon was as calm as Robert Horry shooting the game winning shot. "C'mon OG. You gone sit down or are you just gonna stare at me all night? Be real with me. What you think I don't know, I know." No one had ever made me challenge myself that way he did. Truthfully, it still did bother me til this day. It was something that I had a hard time letting go of. I sat in the chair and scooted it close to the table. I folded my hands on the table and just sat there for a minute, staring at him. He was staring back, now mimicking my sitting stance. The boy indeed was no fool. He knew exactly how to get me going. "January 2016," I began. I couldn't believe that I was about to tell this entire story to someone for the first time in my life.

There I was, riding through this huge, yet empty state on my way back to my alma mater. I had just finished visiting my parents down in North Carolina. They were both now officially veterans. Mom, she had retired years earlier. My dad took his rightful place months earlier among the great Marines of past and present as he was retired with full honors as a Master Gunnery Sergeant. It was heartwarming to see such a thing. That was a long fucking time to serve. I know they were a bit strict growing up, but it turned me into a success story. Over the years, my life had seen me go from being born in California, raised 10 years in North Carolina, went to Montana for college, graduate, move to Miami, then to Portland, spend a month in Boise and now back to Portland. I never liked being in one place for a long time. I always thought that the earth was too big to just stay in one place and be a loaner. I wanted to loan myself to the world. One thing I could say about being a beat writer was that it took me all over. I remember when I told Omarr, or "O" as I called him sometimes, that I wanted to go on a yearlong excursion all over the map. He looked at me like I was nuts. He didn't get what I was trying to do. It was New Year's 2016 and we were all drunker than a skunk when I told him I wanted to travel to 52 places and not be known by a soul bruh. "Man, what the hell are you talking about?," he asked me, champagne steady being sipped from his glass. "I bring 52 different stories to you from 52 different places and we make the magazine turn anew at the top of next year. 52 in 52 could be the name of the article. Think how big that would be? No one, and I mean no one has ever done that. I'll drive my own whip, pay for my own hotels, my food, my toilet paper, all that. I want this man. You gotta trust me." Of course, saying most of that, my speech was slurred, but they say when you are drunk that you usually tell the truth. "Ok man. Well what you gonna do about your place out here?"

"I'm gone rent it out," I told him. "I'll pack seven outfits and head out on the road to live out of a suitcase. Just direct deposit my cash flow to the account and we good."

"Bruh," he said, taking another sip of the champagne in his glass. "I'll front you $100,000. Give you something to spend out there. Just send me everything you can. I wanna see this. Good luck." Truthfully, I don't know why I chose to do this, but I felt it would be a wakeup call for my life. As I got home that night around two in the morning, thanking God that I didn't get pulled over by the Portland PD, I pulled out a map and plotted my routes. I was gonna start by heading south to California. The Bay would be my first stop. There were a couple major cities that I could knock out in one session like Oakland and Frisco. Follow that by heading to Fresno, L.A. and then San Diego. I couldn't wait to hit San Diego. I wanted me a surf-n-turf burrito. I heard they had the best Mexican food known to man. From there, I would head east to Phoenix, Albuquerque and then wherever else I decided. I pondered on how this decision would change my life. Give up everything so that I could find out who I was. I was in my mid 30's. Most 30 something year old's were trying to figure out what would be the next step in their lives. I was simply trying to figure out how in the hell could I be different than the average man. I fell asleep that night at peace, right there on the living room floor. My suit was still on and everything. Ok, truthfully, the liquor started to set in and I passed out on the floor. It didn't have anything to do with being in some peaceful state of mind. I woke up the next day and started to make arrangements with my crib. I found a young intern at the gig who needed somewhere to really get his work done, so I let him use the pad. He covered the rent. I figured I could scrape up the bread for utilities, seeing how he was still young and still trying to up his paycheck. I packed up the toiletries, draws, t-shirts and most of my good clothes. From here on out, it would be me and my whip. Tonight, I would spend the night at Omarr's. Tomorrow, I would head out on a journey that would forever change me. My stop in the Bay was by far the most interesting journey on my entire trip. Frisco was the first stop. Man, the term vibrant was an understatement here. When it came to fashion, it was easy up here. All I had to do was head down to the gay neighborhoods. Frisco was known as the gay capital of America. One thing about a lot of gay people was that they had a mixture of different lifestyles. I felt comfortable around here. I wasn't a homophobe. They were people like me or anyone else. My lifestyle may not have been theirs, but as I said earlier, I treat the CEO with the same respect that I treat the janitor with. I treat the straights with the same respect that I do the gay population. I journeyed to a few restaurants and spots where the gay community frequented. They welcomed me with open arms. I saw all sorts of fashion trends. Some made me say hell naw. Others just made my eyes get big. Either way, it was interesting to say the least. I then mobbed on over to Oakland. I was careful here. Oakland wasn't a town where you just roam around and talk to anyone at will. Oakland was a killing field. So, to be safe, I hit one of my partners from college and had him meet me in downtown Oakland so that I could be gravy on the streets. Oakland was a gritty city. These folks here were hard to the bone. Don't take no mess. Too me, they were like a bunch of civilian Marines. They were as tough as nails. At the same time, they were down to earth. Add in the fact that Chef Curry and crew were doing their thing, and "The Town" as they called it was lit. Fam took me over to West Oakland where some of the pimps and playas roamed. As I looked at these streets, I thought to myself wow, some of the best in the world at their crafts made it out of this city. Gary Payton, Damian Lillard and Marshawn Lynch just to name a few. We stopped at this dim lit brick building on a chill January night. The temperature outside was cold, but it was cooking up in here with some of the baddest women that I had ever seen. Also, some of the flyest brothers I ever seen. The furs and the dead animal skins on their feet were kicking. Shit, I expected PETA to be bugging this joint. My folks introduced me to a cat named G.T. His suit was consisted of different shades of green. Surrounding him on his couch was his hoe collection. I asked money for a few pics. He happily obliged, but not with the females. "No product is put on display for a magazine unless I own the muthafucka," he stated. "That's cool with me pimp juice. I respect the game." After we finished, he took me around and let me interview a bunch of other pimps. This was the Bay. Rather, this was the Yay area. This how they did the damn thing. All I could do was respect it and check it. The next morning, I was headed down to L.A. I figured I could take three days to head down there. I stopped in Fresno for a day and then continued on. Once in the vicinity of the city, I knew where to head, but I had another goal on my mind. I drifted off into Long Beach, so I could see what many considered the mecca of football. GPS was still fresh to my world, but I was making good use of it. There it was. I finally found it. Long Beach Polytechnic High School. Home of the Jackrabbits. Right on the corner of Atlantic and Pacific Coast Highway. Sometimes, I wish I would've grew up in football turf, seeing how I fell in love with it in college. However, it wasn't meant to be. Still, I had to pay homage to this mecca. It wasn't often that you heard of a bunch of inner city kids dominating the football world. I left here and headed back towards Los Angeles, straight into Hollyweird. Boy oh boy. Every type of fashion you could imagine was down here. Truthfully, Hollywood wasn't the nicest of places. I mean, away from the blocks of theatres and stars on the ground, it was some hood life over here. I always made it a purpose to examine where I was at whenever I was doing a shoot or an interview. Fashion is one thing, but if I didn't learn something about the area that I was in, then I was cutting myself short on the learning curve. As I left, I chucked the deuce to the Michael Jackson impersonator on the corner. Boy oh boy, if Gary, Indiana didn't produce anything else, they didn't need to. Michael alone was a greater creation than damn near all of music put together. My last stop in California was down in San Diego. I called Omarr up because I didn't know anyone from around this area. He plugged me with a guy they called Red. I met Red downtown in the Gaslamp. It was an early afternoon as we partook in some drinks at Taste and Thirst. "So where can I get some good shoots for the story?"

"Hillcrest," he responded.

"So, what's it like over there?"

"Rich. Rich as ever. As in culture," he said, sippin whatever he was sippin.

"That's cool with me. I'm comfortable."

"I ain't. I'm a lead the way down there and you call me if you need anything. They got a lot of good eating joints down there, but like I said, I don't fuck with it. Too many wild ass folks down there. Now, either take it or leave it?"

"Trust, I'm good brother. I'm following you. You helping me out." As I tailed him leaving downtown, my mind kind of crossed into another zone. The world was changing indeed. I remember back in the days if you said you were gay, the world crucified you. Now, it was becoming a society norm. I can't necessarily knock someone for their lifestyle. I mean, it's their choice how they want to live it. Key word, choice, because no one is born a certain way. That is the dumbest crap I have ever heard in my life. We can take it away from gays for a minute. So, if a kid grows up and murders 50 people, are we gonna say he was born a murderer? If a young lady grows up and ends up strung out on drugs, are we now gonna say she was born a crack addict? No. Like everything in life, people make choices. I think the whole I was born this way crap was created by people who didn't wanna face the reality of making their own choices. My choice was too remain straight. Their choice was to love someone of the same gender as them. Fine and dandy. I didn't push my beliefs on them and I would hope that they didn't push theirs on me. At the same time, it was no reason to hate them. I made that mistake when I was in high school. There were a few gay kids in my school. One in particular was so flamboyant and always running his yap about me and my partners that I wanted to smash his head in at times. I didn't like gays and I was a huge homophobe. It's amazing how time changes things. See, some people age and others grow. Just because a man is 50, does not mean he is 50 in the mind. Then you may have a man who is 50, yet his mental tells you he is 100, because he has expanded beyond the numerics of his age. Fashion was one thing, but we needed to pay attention to people. Fat women aren't my preference and I rarely find them attractive. However, if a fat woman just so happens to be the surgeon who is gonna save my life, I am surely not going to tell her that I don't want her to operate on me. I am not fond of sushi, but if I am homeless, I will not deny the handout from the Japanese restaurant owner who is attempting to feed me. I damn sure ain't a fan of the Padres, because I was a diehard Chicago Cubs fan and will be til I die. However, if one of these great San Diegans offered me tickets to Petco Park, I would surely go. See if we started to look at each other as people, instead of the individual, then the world would run much smoother. Still don't get what I am saying? Check this out. This individual, me, loves certain things. The person, me, myself, is respectful and carries himself well. Who gives a rat's ass what some people like or dislike? If they are a good person, then they should be treated as such, regardless of choice of lifestyle, ethnicity, skin color, any of that. I enjoyed Hillcrest for all that it had that day. The vibrancy of the section, the people and especially, the good food. If I had a recommendation, I would say try Hash

House a Go Go. I caught them an hour before close and it was one of the best decisions I ever made in my life. I got back to my hotel that night on Harbor Drive and just relaxed in style. Having a view of the Pacific Ocean and all these ships was indeed soothing. In two days, I would depart here and began my trek East. Through all the stops that I would make, none would be better than when I finally touched down in Raleigh, North Carolina, where my now retired Marine parents resided. I knew they were proud of me, as I was of them. I just wanted them to see the results of what they worked so hard to provide for. Phoenix was indeed intriguing. Albuquerque was dry, desolate, but gave you enough flare to be considered as a major city. Austin has 6th street. Dallas, well, I really didn't have anything wrong to say about Dallas. H-Town, well, I really didn't have anything wrong to say about H town. College Station, well, I really didn't have anything bad to say about College Station either. As a matter of fact, I had nothing bad at all to say about Texas period. I just wanted to know one thing. What in the hell were they putting in the water down there? No girl that I saw had a flat booty. There was nothing but a bunch of plump bump rumps roaming around. Now, I was a booty man and there was enough of that down there to stop all world feuds. Even ol' boy in North Korea would calm down if he saw what those Texas girls were dragging on their backsides. Then, I hit Shreveport, Louisiana. As quick as I hit that place, I skedaddled out of that place. Ratchet was an understatement. Continuing East, I got to what I considered a city that built people into tough ones. Baton Rouge. All I could think about here was the purple and yellow feel of Death

Valley, as Saturdays turned this place into a madhouse. With a connect from one of my college buddies down here, I was able to shoot some of the football players in their different styles of dress from around the country. I really don't know why folks were trying to bring the 80's back, but it was happening. I couldn't do snapbacks anymore. Those days were long gone and I wanted to keep them there. I respected it, but it wasn't me anymore. After staying two nights and catching a LSU basketball game versus Ole Miss, I continued on until I got to New Orleans, or Nawlins as us black folks called it. This was my first time here and my first stop was the French Quarter. Ah man, New Orleans. What could I say about this place? Rather what could I not say about this place? It had everything you wanted. The live jazz music thumping up and down the street made your heart dance to its own rhythm in your chest. The smell of crawfish, gumbo, shrimp, that classic Creole cooking just made your nose orgasm about twenty times. I sat atop numerous buildings inside of the French Quarter for two days, snapping photos and interviewing random people. Hell, I even saw Juvenile while I was here. He was walking through just enjoying himself. New Orleans was on one I tell you. But, but, it was another side to this city that I had to see. The one that was all too often broadcast on television. It was the dark side of the N.O. Me being me, the next day, I got up early at around five o'clock and hooked up with my connect happily named "Trap." He showed me what every black person in America wanted to see but was kept from view. He showed me every spot where the government intentionally had the levees destroyed. You talk about a land grab. This was more like a free for all contest to see who could obtain the most in the shortest amount of time. I didn't even look at the Superdome as the home of the Saints. I saw it as a refuge for the many residents who were trying to escape Hurricane Katrina. Notice I said residents and not refugees. How the hell could you be called a refugee in the same country that you were born and raised in? It was complete and utter garbage to know D.C. would treat folks like this. Then again, you had to see who was in office at the time. He ain't give a damn and neither did his daddy. Gentrification was the name of the tactic and they executed it with precision. In that moment, I started to shun my parents a little bit. I know they weren't directly involved in it, seeing that they were never stationed here. However, the military was used to cause a major part of this destruction. I believe that is another reason why I never joined. Seeing the camaraderie was one thing. However, I didn't want to be part of something that may force you to impede on the will of others to satisfy an agenda. Not shitting on the military, because a lot of those brothers and sisters are positive. However, the powers to be that control them have little to no hearts a lot of the time. I left the homey Trap with major understanding about the folks of New Orleans and continued on East through Mississippi and Alabama. I didn't stop in either one of those states. Nothing against the great people of those states, but the history of those two places just rubbed me the wrong way. Next up was Tallahassee, Florida. Luckily, I had lived in this state previously, so I didn't have to wonder what the Florida life was like. I, however, didn't know anything about Tallahassee except for T-Pain. The boy had hits and put this city on something serious.

I will say, however, his hit song "Buy U A Drank" had girls upset at me. They would hear that and approach me asking for a drink. I buy you a drink and you buying this dick right along with it was my mindset back in the day. Let's face it, all women head to these nightspots thinking that they are the baddest things walking the face of the earth. See, they know all men gone peep 'em out. Trust, though, it ain't for their looks necessarily. Men, especially those of an elder age, realize that a vagina is attached to every woman. The primary goal of all men is to get in the draws to test those waters. So, the way I worked it was if they wanted to drink with me, either they buy it themselves and come chill, or my twelve dollars for some crown and coke was gonna include a night session after twelve o'clock. That's just how it was. As I cruised this city, I passed by Florida State. The memories of watching Charlie Ward growing up along with the legion of Seminole legends had me spellbound. Even though I was diehard purple and orange when it came to football, I had to give respect where respect was due. Then, as I kept driving, I saw that another university sat almost directly across the street from FSU. It was FAMU. Florida A&M University. It was an historically all black college. Boy, the damage I would have done if I would have went here instead of Montana. It's a good thing I didn't. All this chocolate in one place was too much for me. I would've either left with ten kids or ten STD's. I kept it around the college area, strolling into local coffee shops and cafés, talking to students about where they were from and the culture that they represented. I even met a few who were supposedly part of the new Black Panther Party."

"And then everything stopped. Right?" I looked at Twon, trying to keep my emotions in check. "How'd you know?"

"I read one of the old magazines that you kept in your bedroom closet. I saw the condolences to your father. Saw that you lost him during the road trip. See you tell me about starting anew. But truthfully. If you ask me. OG. I don't think you ever started over. I think you have been living outside of the truth. Not saying your life is a lie, but it seems like you got some soul searching to do yourself." It was crazy how those younger than us could sometimes know much more than we could.

— 4 —

TRUTH SESSION #3

"HELLO?"

"It's almost time man. I know you ready to come back." As excited as I thought I would be when this conversation finally happened, there was not a joyous bone in my body at all.

"Hello?"

"Yeah I'm still here."

"Why you sounding so sad man? I know you ain't become attached to North Dakota. I know you ain't about to tell me that. Let me guess. You met a bad ass snow bunny up there huh?"

"Naw bruh. It's not that. I'm attached to this kid man." Just then I heard the key going into the lock. "Let me call you back Paul," I said really fast, hanging up on him while he was in mid-sentence. "Yo what's up OG?" I cracked a smile at Twon, sweating bullets in the process, with a racing heart.

"Yo you good? You look like you just ran on the cardio machine."

"Oh nah. I'm good. Old friend from back in the day called me and she kinda made my heart skip a beat."

"Uh oh," Twon said, as he plopped down on the couch and placed his bag on the floor. "Thinking about flying her out here?"

"With what money?"

"I mean hell. Greyhound. Skateboard. Something." That actually made me laugh a little bit. "A, I'm a go take a shower man. I got some good news to share with you when I get out."

"Aight man." Twon literally skipped his ass into the bathroom and shut the door. Whatever had happened to him today, it had him on ten. I waited a bit at the kitchen table, waiting for the shower water to kick on. I pulled my phone back out and returned the call to Paul, the then intern that I lent my place to two years ago. As it rang, a lightbulb went off in my head and I walked outside, shutting the door behind me.

"Man, why you hang up on me?"

"Ok man look. Man. So I met this kid right. He was down on his luck man, and I kind of took him in."

"Ok, so what does this have to do with anything?"

"He doesn't know the truth man. And the kid looks at me as damn near a father figure. He gone be crushed man. This nigga really believes I'm poor." Things got silent for about five seconds on the phone. "Hello," I said to Paul. "I'm here man. I'm here. Well, all I gotta say is this. You can either let him down hard or let him down easy."

"C'mon bruh. This shit ain't that simple."

"Yes, man I know. But you sacrificed a year of your life for a lifetime of bread. You were already set. Now your grandkids, grandkids gone be set for life. That kid will be aight."

"Damn man. Thanks for the honest words," I told him so sarcastically.

"Hey man. Rather have honesty than bullshit. I'll see you in two weeks bruh."

"Ok man."

"Gone." I walked back in the house, crushed inside, but not showing it on my face.

"Sup OG. Where you go?"

"Just stepped outside for some air man. That's all."

"Yeah I'm glad it's actually feeling kind of summerish around here. You know Midwest weather likes to stay bipolar for a while."

"Damn man. Where you going?," I asked him. "You showered fast, got some jeans and a polo on. Do I know this young man?" He laughed, but I noticed something a little different with this laugh. He had a glow behind it. It was a laugh that was genuine. It was from the heart. "Ok man. So, two things. One, I got a job. Two," as he threw up the deuces. "I got a job man."

"Oh shit," I said, flopping down on the couch and stretching my left arm out. "I'm proud of you man," I told him, extending my hand out as he walked up and gave me dap. "So, where's the job at?"

"It's a late-night janitor at a school about three blocks down from here. I go in tonight at seven and I'm off at one. Ten dollars an hour, five days a week. I'd figure it's a stepping stone towards the right direction. You know. An honest man's pay. Just like you." I shook my head up and down, closing my eyes. Deep down, I wanted to cry as my inner soul was eating me alive at this point. Outside, I couldn't show that feeling on my face. I looked at my watch to see that it was ten past six. "Well," I said. "You better get going don't you think?"

"It's three blocks down. I'll leave at 6:20 and get there with time to spare. Yo," as he pulled out a chair from the kitchen table. "I was wondering when you were gonna sit down," I told him. "Look. OG." He paused for a minute, collecting himself, trying to prevent himself from crying. "I just wanna say. Man, I appreciate it. You took a chance on me when it felt like everyone else in this world gave up on me. I won't let you down." I continued to listen and feel lower than dirt as he continued on. "I mean hell. Look at us. We might be broke. But this here," as he waved his finger back and forth between us. "This right here. This is rich. Money couldn't buy this connection. I got love for you OG." At that moment, my heart sank. Twon got up and we embraced in a hug. "Go head and get to ya job man," I said softly to him, eyes watery as hell. "Yo you crying OG?"

"Naw man. Naw. Got some dust in my eye." We both got a laugh out of that. Twon turned around and walked towards the door. As he opened it, he looked back at me. "Oh, I forgot something." He reached in his back pants pocket and tossed me a pack of Top Ramen noodles. "I paid for these. Just wanted to make amends for my mistake." He chucked the deuce and headed out the door. I collapsed on the floor. I was dropping tears. You would've thought that both of my parents died in a train wreck by the way I was crying. I wasn't a man, and my soul was pretty much dead. My lies had not yet come out in the physical, but the shameful truth was here, and I had a decision to make.

The drinks were flowing on that chilly Friday night in downtown Portland. The company had hit a new milestone. We had broken a new record for profit, and it saw all of its employees collect huge bonuses. Myself, I had a check that sung to the tune of $300,000. It was amazing how the fashion and entertainment industry worked. You simply write articles, chase down the latest news in fashion and expose it to the world. All of a sudden, everything is gravy with no rice. "Darnell." I turned around to see O come next to me, putting his arm around me. "Sup my dude?"

"Yo, I just wanna tell you some shit, and this ain't the Hennessey talking." That's how I really knew that it was the Hennessey talking. "I just wanna say in front of all these white people in Portland and all this weird shit up here, and all this terrible music they have playing in here. We did it man. We did it. You my ace boon coon hands down."

"I'll toast to that my dude," as I held my glass of champagne up. He held his up and we clinked glasses in midair, tossing back this strong, yet smooth ass liquid in a glass. "Man, what is this shit you custom ordered for tonight?," I asked him. "It's called the liquid blunt," he responded. "You been watching Eddie Griffin again huh?"

"Hey man. This the shit he must've been talking about when he talked about fucking a fat, raggedy ass bitch. He said bubbles for your troubles. Well this shit here, can make any man fuck anything with no problems at all. Shit, I'm ready right now. I'll lie a big girl down, lift up one of her rolls and long stroke that ass while collecting the loose change that's been sitting in the pits of her stomach for years." I literally spit my drank out and laughed so hard at the damn bar when he said that. O went back off into the night and I just sat there, greeting the folks who would come up to me every few minutes and congratulate me on my success. It was crazy how the magazine exploded from this Pac Northwest city. It wasn't Hollywood to say the least, but we exploited the city to a point where people assumed we had the Hollywood flare. We bounced to the tune of old 80's hip hop and the modern shit playing through the speakers for the rest of the night. Once one in the morning hit, I was beyond tired. My buzz had worn off due to the many glasses of water I had drunk within the last hour. I got up, chucking the deuce in the air to everyone who could see me. Trying to be indiscreet as possible, I mobbed out the back door of the joint. I loved the folks I worked with, but I really didn't wanna see any of 'em on the way out. Not to mention that my car was in the back lot behind the building as well. "It's nice being rich huh?" Immediately, I inserted the key in my door and reached for the side door. If there was anyone who was playing games, this glock would cure their troubles. "You don't need that man. I ain't on that shit." I looked around. It literally sounded like this voice was coming from every direction. The parking lot was lit, but still somewhat dim. "Yo, I ain't trying to be on no kill shit, but I will shoot you." I literally was spinning around while saying that. This was a scene out of one of those creepy ass mystery movies. I couldn't see where this person was at. "Then shoot me." I turned around to see a shadow emerging in the little light that emitted from behind the building. Once he came into view, I saw a slender brother in a navy-blue pinstripe suit, rocking a fedora with a red band. It was like looking at candy man mixed with an old pimp who didn't know he wasn't a pimp anymore. My gun was up, ready to fire. "If you were gonna shoot me, you would've did it by now." He literally walked up and met his chest with my glock. "Who are you?," I asked, with my finger steady on the trigger. "I'm the boogeyman," he said, leaning his head to the right, hands firmly locked in front of him. "What you want man? Don't play. I will lay yo ass down."

"Will you Darnell?" My eyebrows raised. This dude actually knew my name. "Now," as he took his hand and guided the gun down. "Chill. I know everything about you." A smirk came across my face. "Congrats nigga. You know my name. Now stop playing games. Who are you? I don't hear the music coming out of the building. No commotion. Nice job. Big O put you up to this. Ha ha. Nice joke, but I don't do games my dude. Leave me the fuck alone. I'm going home." I turned around and walked back towards my car. "Running is something you were always good at. Much like you ran from Miami to here." I stopped dead in my tracks, turned around and looked dead at him. "Who are you man?," I asked him again, walking up to him, stopping dead in front of him. "I'm God. I knew you before you were created. I knew you when you were born. I know the moment you gone die. But, it won't be now cause I ain't done with you yet." I literally began to laugh out loud. "Yo, my dude," as I continued to laugh hysterically. "Man, Omarr a fucking fool for this one. Good one my dude. What's your name playa?" I threw my right hand in the air wanting him to dap me up, but he just stood there and looked at me. "Yo, for real man. It's all good now. You just gone leave me hanging?" He turned around and took two steps towards the door. He stopped and looked up to the sky. "What good is it that a man gains the entire earth and loses his soul in the process?," he said. Then, he turned back around. "But what if I asked you. Would a man be willing to die to give someone else a life they have never seen?" I was now tired of this dude. He had taken a joke too far. "Aight my dude. Look. Whatever shit you on, get some help my dude. I'm out." I turned around to walk back to the car. That's when I heard the music coming from inside again. I turned around and looked. Dude was gone. I just shook my head. Either I was already sleep and dreaming really bad, or one of those drinks had really messed me up. I turned back towards the car and my heart began to immediately pound out of my chest as I dropped my keys. The slender dude was now leaning on my driver side door. "I told you," he said, with a silly grin. He took the few steps up towards me, meeting me face to face. "I'm God. Nigga. And trust. Saying nigga is the only way you gone believe me. Now let me tell you something. My son went into the wilderness for 40 days and 40 nights. Gave up everything when he could've just took the easy road out. Now, I'm gone give you a chance. Give it all up for one year. Leave it all behind to humble yourself. And son, I'll give you everything you ever dreamed of and more. It's your choice. Your choice." He began to walk away towards the darkness. "**WAIT!!!**," I yelled. He turned around. "How I know I ain't drunk and just hallucinating with all of this?" The slender man smirked, reaching in his pocket. He tossed me something and I caught it. I opened my hand to see a quarter. "And in Luke it said therefore I tell you, do not worry about your life, what you will eat; or about your body, what you will wear. For life is more than food, and the body more than clothes. Think about it." I just looked at him as he rose his hand and snapped his fingers. All the lights in the lot went out. In the blink of an eye, they came back on and he was gone. The music could be heard again. I was stuck in a trance. I looked down at my watch. As long as that experience had seemed to last, only five minutes had passed. The door then flew open. "Yo. Nigga. What you been doing out here?" I raised my head up to see that it was Omarr, drunk as a skunk, slurring in my face.

"Yo, I'm good man."

"You gone come back in and party?"

"Nah man. I'm headed home."

"Shit," he said, leaning like a heroin addict in a hurricane. "A look man. We gotta talk tomorrow."

"Ok?" The look on my face said it all. His eyes were closed the whole time he said that. Before I could get out another word, he began to fall forward. Luckily, I caught him, but he was a little heavy to be holding up. I just eased him down gently on the ground. I know it wasn't the classiest thing to do, but he could dry clean that suit later. He was now snoring, and I just stood over him, with a little smirk on my face. "We'll talk tomorrow bruh," I told him, leaned over. I turned around and walked back to my car, peeling off into the night.

———————————

"Hello?"

"Yo man what's good?"

"Oh, snaps man. You don't even sound like you hungover."

"Man bruh. I woke up on the ground, with people all around me. I was fucked up." I laughed at that, and the convo went into the magazine and ideas we had. This Saturday evening was chill and everything was normal. "Yo, I wanna know how dedicated you are to me?" I literally pulled the phone away and looked at it. I know this dude wasn't about to come out of the closet and tell me that he loved me. "Man, what is wrong with you?"

"Everything man. Look. A few months ago, my mentor was diagnosed with chronic heart disease. They done gave him one or two years tops, but he wanna give you a whole lot more." I ain't even take my guy serious. I really thought he was bullshitting. "Aight man. What you need man? Cut the bullshit."

"You gotta go live in North Dakota for a year." Now I knew he was trippin. "Aight bruh. I got it. What's poppin' out there? We wanna expand to them country ass folks? Tell me who I'm going to see?" All was quiet on the phone for a good 15 seconds. "Hello?"

"Yeah I'm here."

"Talk then man. For real. Who I'm going to see out there? What's the fashion line?"

"Bruh. My mentor. He from there. He dying. He too damn rich. He wanna give his money away."

"And this has what to do with me?"

"Aight fuck it. One year in North Dakota. One year in a modest one bedroom. Live off of three grand a month. You do that. Fifty million nigga. **FIFTY, FUCKING, MILLION!!!**" Now my ears were free of wax and the doors of the church were open. I knew when my dude was serious. "Bruh. Like. Why me?"

"Because he's followed your work. He knows you've earned everything that you have received. Every award, accolade, praise, all that shit. This a damn near billionaire bruh. This ain't a game. Now you in or you out?"

I called Paul back. This was indeed the most uncomfortable call back in my life. Now, he wasn't answering the phone and I was more nervous than a chicken crossing the road with some bruhs barbecuing on the other side. I glanced down at my watch. "Shit. I'm gonna be late," I said out loud. My weekly meeting time was approaching and here I was, still in the house, lollygagging around. I threw on some sweats and a thermal, and charged it to the game. As I arrived at the center where we met, to my surprise, I didn't see Cleavon's car. That was odd in my opinion. He was always the first one here. He always had this saying that if you were on time, you were late. If you were early, then you were on time. I got out the car, wondering what could be holding him up. I saw Byron's car and Lamont's. Walking towards the door and getting a glance around the corner of the building, I could see Kelvin mom's car. Everyone was here, but where the hell was Cleavon? I walked inside the building, removing my hat as I walked to the room. Through the window, I saw Cleavon, looking at me with his glasses down on his face. "Man, I thought you weren't here. I ain't see ya car outside." I took my seat. Everyone was simply staring at me. "Whoa man. What the hell is y'all staring at?" I looked around the room and then back to Cleavon. "You know since you finally made it. On time, might I add. Lemme ask you something. What's the difference between Lebron and Kevin Durant?" I was confused as all to be damned. "Bruh. like what is you talking about? Ain't we supposed to be talking about life?"

"We are talking about life. Now, tell me what's the difference between Lebron James and Kevin Durant?" I figured he was trying to go somewhere with this, so I said the only thing I could think of. "Nothing Cleavon. Absolutely not a damn thing." Cleavon glasses came down beneath his eyes again, as if to say I was wrong, or did you just say what I think you said.

"So why you say that?"

"Cause they grown ass men."

"Are you crazy?," Lamont chimed in.

"Naw fool I ain't. And by the way. Cleavon. Again, what is the point of this?"

"You worry about yo convo with Lamont. I'll tell you why later." I just shook my head and looked back at Lamont. "Man look," Lamont said. "He married his Black high school sweetheart, sent many kids to college in Ohio, he helped the city of Cleveland, he can go anywhere he wants to make his money as a young Black man." The rest of us looked around at each other as Cleavon was still in his chair with those rainbow-colored socks, laughing his ass off. "Man, what the fuck is you talking about man?," I asked him. "Man here me out. If you know anything about life, you will know winning is not everything. Cleveland is good. The city is thriving more and more. Lebron's personal life is in Ohio where he has made an impact. Who cares about a national loss? The Cavs still did well. His money will always be in Ohio. The city is not dead. Cleveland, Ohio is poppin' by the way. By the way, people in Cali are doing bad. Y'all can't even afford to live in Cali. Most people have to move out to survive. At least if you're educated you can afford to eat and live well in Cleveland. We got jobs and affordable housing, unlike Cali. Have a stadium full of seats." At that point, I began to severely laugh because the shit was beyond funny. Through my watery eyes, I could see Cleavon was now leaned over in his seat, hollin. Kelvin was Kelvin, holding his mother's hand, shaking, oblivious to this whole conversation. Byron just had his arms folded, shaking his head. "Aight, aight," Cleavon said, calming down and coming back to reality. "Exactly what you said Lamont, is the reason why I started this convo. And you, my friend, sound retarded as shit."

"What you mean old man? I told the truth. You say we here to uplift and connect with each other, then you say I'm retarded. Well what makes you the great thinker? Huh?" Lamont had now raised up out of his seat. "Lamont," as Cleavon had now put his glasses back on straight and kept his sitting stance. "Twenty-Two Twelve."

"What?"

"Twenty-two twelve." Lamont sat back down. "What the hell are you talking about old man?"

"What I'm talking about is the fact that don't think cause I'm an old man now who moves a little slower than usual that I won't go medieval Vice Lord on your ass. I asked you a question but understand where I'm from. Where I'm from. You raise up on a man, then you better pull up on him. See you hollin this shit about the land. The only land I know about is the motherland, which we been calling that shit for decades now. No NBA player had to come and put it on a jersey to start getting brothers to say it. Now I'm gone tell you something else, and this is what really matters. And I want all y'all knuckleheads to listen. Kelvin, you with me?"

"Ye...Ye...Yes sir?"

"Alright now. Smoke this over. At one point, both those men left what they knew to achieve a goal. Now you can call them what you want, but the fact is your opinion don't matter. All y'all here, including my old ass. See it's easy to talk shit in your little settings, or your notebook, Facebook, sky book or whatever the fuck social media they got right now. But guess what, we do the same shit in everyday life. How would you feel if every time you went to get a better job, with better qualified people, that someone brought up your past? Oh, you couldn't make it. Oh, you sold out your community. Oh, you went to prison. Well guess what? I did more time than all you negroes combined, came back out to a Chicago that made Iraq look like a safe haven, and I chose to surround myself with better people, better opportunity and better time management, all so I could achieve a goal. But some of you too stupid to see that. See pride. Pride is the reason that people don't make it. You always wanna be in competition with each other. Wanna one up the next man. Oh sure. We talk big, but we ain't shit in the bigger picture. See we're not just men. **WE ARE BLACK MEN!!!** We are born with two strikes. Nobody hates a man. They hate his skin. They try to overlook and justify their bullshit done on the stolen land which they snatched away and tried to push the shit that they created off on you like a cult, and get mad if you not for their ways, and you're considered a threat if you're not for what they call America. That's my answer. I asked you gentlemen a long time ago. What is the square root of pain. **THAT'S THE SQUARE ROOT OF PAIN!!!** Competition. And Lamont, I don't know where the fuck you come off talkin reckless about Cali, cause you from that muthafucka." We were all quiet. I, in particular, didn't know what to say. OG had just broken life down in basketball terms, something that we could all understand. This was a Cleavon that I had never seen before. He had fire in his eyes and hell in his voice. "And lastly. If you wanna know what the square root of bullshit is, then take in Lamont's words. Muthafucka the question ain't have shit to do with living conditions, schools, or none of that. That's shit said by muthafuckas who can't win an argument. What you got Lebron's dick in ya mouth or some shit? Ya dumb ass talked about ya own home state that you from. You left, so you must be shitty too huh? You know what. Fuck this. I'm gone. Y'all can sit around here and talk for the next hour or so. I don't give a shit what y'all do. I'm going home. Just know if any of you ever stand up on me again, I may not swing anymore,

111

but I can damn sure shoot." He lifted up his long button up to expose a small pistol, showing it to everyone in the room. Cleavon smooth walked out the door and down the hall. We all just sat there for the next five minutes not saying one word. "Hey man," as Byron broke the silence. "Yo, I ain't never had no shit in life broke down to me like that. Man. I gotta go man."

"Where you going B?," I asked him. He turned around at the door. "Man, after some shit like that, I gotta go home and make some pork chops with Cajun seasoning for my boys. Shit made me think and hungry." Byron walked out. Kelvin, about a minute later, his mom helped him up with his dreadful shaking and they walked out. It was just me and Lamont left now. We just sat there for another five minutes, not knowing what to do. Finally, I had enough of the silent treatment. "So, you wanna talk brother?"

"Naw man. I'm taking my talents somewhere else."

"What you mean?," I asked him as he raised up out of his seat.

"That's all I needed to hear. I don't need this no more. I got my mind focused now. I'm moving back to California."

"But why man? Why?," I asked him, confused.

"I feel like it's easy to be the best player when you don't have good players around you. I feel like it's harder to stand out when you have great players around you. I pride myself on standing out wherever I am. I pride myself on working hard wherever I go. And I feel like these guys embraced me and I feel like I'm a Warrior."

"So now you think you Kevin Durant huh? A minute ago you were tryna defend Lebron."

"Well," he said, scratching his head. "After what Cleavon said, he made me think. It's easy to be the man out here. Get out of prison, work in the oil fields and make good money. But this ain't me dawg. I'm from the bright lights, the glitz and glam. We all ended up out here to get away. But, how long can you run away from your true self man? The answer is you can't. Oil fields, hard labor. This ain't me. I was a screenwriter before I got hooked on the drugs. Now I ain't making an excuse, but I was young and didn't know how to think for myself. But now, now I do. I'm going back to L.A. man. I can only get better by being around those who do better. I'll see you when I see you man." Lamont left out the room and it was just me. What I thought was gonna be an hour-long talk ended up being me alone in a room with 45 minutes left before I originally had planned to leave. I just sat there, looking around the room. I got up and started walking around, looking at the random books that were scattered out and about. Nothing in particular caught my eye, that was until I glanced down at the bottom of one of the tables. Underneath it, was a book covered in so much dust that I know it had to have been written during the dinosaur era. I bent down to pick it up and blew the dust off. "Damn," I said, coughing along the way. Yeah, I was stupid. I should've expected all that to flame through the air. I took a rag that I always carried in my back pocket and wiped it off. Looking thoroughly, I saw the writing that was on the cover was nearly gone. The only thing that was left was the black leather. I opened it up and it literally fell apart. The pages and everything crumpled to the floor, and I just left it there. As I began to walk out, something told me to go look through those pages one time. An unseen energy was pulling me. I don't know, but it got me. I went back and just snatched up one page off the floor. I blew the dust off it, again, which was an idiotic mistake. I dusted and there I saw one line that stood out. "Every man wants to live, but don't nobody wanna die." I dropped the paper back down to the floor. I didn't need any subliminal messages for the day. I walked out and simply went back to my car. I got home and just sat in the whip for a minute. A lot of stuff was running through my mind. In particular, how would I break the news to this kid who looked up to me that I was perhaps the biggest fraud of them all? It wasn't easy, but eventually, I would have to face the fire and risk burning. I got out the car. "**YO OG!!!**" I turned around to see it was Twon. He was running up to me from across the street. "What you doing here man? Thought you didn't get off til the wee hours of the morning."

"Man, I'm blessed yo. I had been working so hard that boss man gave me the next two days off and peep." He said peep and flashed a wad of cash in my face.

"How much is that?"

"$200. You know what I can do with this?"

"Hopefully something smart." I turned to walk up the stairs. This was all too much for me right now. "Yo, what's wrong OG?," I heard Twon ask me, as he followed me up. He walked in and shut the door behind him. "Be honest with me man. I mean, you always 100 with me. What happened?"

"You want something to drink Twon?"

"Knowledge OG. That's all I'm trying to drink right now. I got legal money, I'm progressing in life. Not at a fast pace, but it's a pace nonetheless. Just break me off with what's going on in your mental right now." He plopped down on the couch as I stood in the kitchen just staring at him. "Aight man. Hold on. Lemme pour up some of this cranberry juice." I took my time, because I had a decision to make. Either lie big or lie small. Either way, I was gonna lie. I came back in the room, with a glass for both of us.

"Man appreciate you OG."

"Yeah, not a problem," I said, as I handed him the glass and pulled up one of the chairs from my makeshift kitchen table. "Aight look. I gotta head up to Portland for a week." Twon looked at me crazy. "Portland. Oregon or Maine?"

"Does it matter?"

"I mean yeah it kind of do. Both places filled with white folks. Go to one, you at least got a decent chance of living. Go to another, you'll probably get nigga lynched."

"And you assume this how?"

"I mean c'mon OG. The Trailblazers. At least them white folks up there are used to seeing brothers going in and out with the NBA. Portland, Maine? It's a few, and I mean few. I know where I would wanna take my chances at," he said, as he took another gulp from his glass. I didn't say anything on his words, but the little youngster was right. Portland, Oregon was extremely weird, but you had a better chance up there than the other joint. "I'm going for some recruitment business."

"Ain't that's what they got scouts for OG?" He caught me red handed.

It was think quick mode. "Ok look. I'm going for a coaching seminar and I'm tryna get a few heads while I'm up there on the sneak tip. That better?" Deep down, I hope it was. "Aww you on some sneaky shit huh?," Twon said, wagging his finger. "Yeah man. Hey. Gotta do what you gotta do." We laughed over that and I drank my juice nervously.

"When you leaving?"

"Saturday bruh. You got the crib for a week. Now, I only got three rules. You bring someone in here, change the sheets before I get back. Two, don't do anything to bring the police over here. I already ain't got much, and I damn sure don't need Fargo P.D. taking the little that I do have. Three, don't touch my car."

"Aww OG c'mon. What if I gotta go cross town or take care of some business or something?"

"Better cross yo ass to them shoes on yo feet and walk. Now I'm serious Twon. This yo one chance to hold it down while I'm gone. Do not. I repeat. Do not fuck this up. Got me?" He looked away with a smirk on his face. "Hello. I asked you a question young brother."

"Man, I got you. No worries. But, damn man. This sound like my mama house."

"Look here mane," as I got up and headed to the kitchen for now a glass of water. "This how the world works. You get ya own shit, you live by ya own rules. You live in someone else's shit, or work for someone else, it's their rules. That's life. You can do for self, or you can do for someone else. Which one do you want?"

"I mean you the same way," he responded. "You working for someone else. I don't see you with a business. No millions. No high-class lifestyle." I took a huge gulp. "You right. You don't. But everything that the light touches in this kingdom, this right here, belongs to me."

"Huh?"

"Yeah I see yo young ass don't even know The Lion King. Just don't fuck up while I'm gone." I went into the room and started to pack up my clothes. Young buck had pissed me off, but I didn't lash out. I just simply got my basic needs together. I had a whole stash at my crib out in Portland. Cars, money, all that. Then, that's when it hit me again. I still had to face the young brother with the truth. More importantly, I had to face my damn self. **"YO TWON!!!"** I heard no response. **"TWON!!!"** Still, no response. "Where in the good hell is this kid?," I whispered to myself, heading back into the living room. He wasn't anywhere in sight. I opened the door to see him walking down the street. Where he was going, I had no idea. However, he would be aight. Me, I truly wouldn't be until I faced my own demons. The time would come for that. In the meantime, it was time for preparations to head back to Rip City.

— 5 —

TRUTH SESSION #4

I LANDED AT PDX at 11:20 a.m., which was 45 minutes ahead of schedule. I don't know what it was about Southwest Airlines, but those foolios always arrived early and never crashed. Sure, you weren't gonna get shit but some peanuts and half a can of juice in the air, but you would damn sure get to your destination on time. I can't even lie. It was good to be back. I had definitely done my thing out here since I touched down from Miami. I strolled through the airport. Everyone else was fast paced, probably in a hurry to make their business accommodations. I was home. No need to rush. I took in the airport of all places. When you leave home, the smallest things become such an aura to you. "**YO!!! WASSUP BOY!!!**" It was Omarr, screaming at baggage claim, arms up like he was signaling for a touchdown. "What's good partna?," I responded, as I dapped my man's up.

"Yo, don't tell me you got a gaggle of shit."

"The fuck is you talking about man?"

"You ain't got three or four bags do you? I'm old bruh. My back ain't made for this shit anymore."

"Man, you only a year older than me."

"I know and that equates to a whole lot more fucking too." All I could do was laugh. "I try to tell you man. Don't be putting yo back into these broads man. I ain't with all that effort shit. A good fifty pumps and I'm good."

"Damn man you ain't gone even get in her guts?," I asked him.

"Man fuck all that. I get mines and then I'm like the Raptors in the playoffs."

"The Raptors in the playoffs?"

"High expectations, but always out by the second round." It's crazy how my guy had a way with words. We continued to chop it up until my bags came about ten minutes later on the carousel. I grabbed both of them and started to wheel one. That's when I saw Omarr walking away. "**A MAN!!!**," I shouted. "You ain't gone help a brother out?"

"Man, I told you my back fucked up. You got muscles big swole. Wheel that shit on." I shook my damn head. Dark skinned muthafuckas I tell you. I wheeled my joints all the way to the parking lot and had to stop when I saw my baby. "Yo, for real man," I said with the biggest grin on my face. Omarr turned around, dangling my keys in the air, with the damn tequila Jordan face. "You ain't think I was gonna let you come back home and not have your baby waiting for you, did you?" I gave two damns about wheeling those bags now. There she was. My Lac truck. Metallic navy blue with tint all over. I swear my Oregon plates never looked cleaner. Omarr popped the back open and threw me the keys. I took my bags and tossed 'em in, then headed over to the driver's seat. Right before I got in, I looked down at my tires. "Da fuck," I said to myself. "Yo man. Who put them thangs on my whip? Them ain't the joints I had when I left."

"I mean shit. It's the least I could do while you were gone man. Get ya shit right so when you came home you could be riding clean."

"My hitta," I told him, as I dapped him up and proceeded to start up the whip. It felt good to drive back in Oregon. It wasn't the ideal place where you thought of black people living, but it was a good amount of us up here. Like they say. Brothers is everywhere. I hit the light right before the freeway as some old Mac Dre was blasting through my speakers. I glanced around the car while O was bobbing his head to the beat. I looked at the dash, then did a double take. "Yo bruh. Really?"

"Ahh shit," O said. "My bad. Ya shit looked so good that I had to floss it around a couple of times. Damn near look better than mines."

"Well shit you could've at least put some gas in this muthafucka."

"MAN, YOU STILL ON A QUARTER TANK!!!"

"That ain't the point negro. You could've at least had this joint on three quarters. Three quarters and a dime bag. Three fifths of Hennessey. Something. I don't like riding on no quarter tank," I told him, as I pulled off from the light and hit the freeway.

"Well damn dog. I'm sorry. Hit the gas station and I'll fill it up."

"I know *** damn well you gone fill it up."

"This dude."

"This dude my ass. This like me spending the night at yo house and eating up two whole packs of bacon and leaving you two uncooked slices."

"C'mon bruh. You gone really remind me of what Deron did that day?"

"Yeah man. That shit was funny." I was laughing my ass off, but Omarr wasn't. Me and the homey Deron had spent the night at his condo one night because we had a business meeting in the early hours of the morning. Like, 6 a.m. early. Instead of driving into downtown and battling the morning rush of the midweek traffic, we crashed at O's house that night. Now, me and that dude both sleep like bricks, but Deron don't. Long story short, O had two packs of bacon. When we arose at 4:30 in the morning, we smelled bacon. We thought that brother had cooked for everyone in the house. Nah. When we got in the kitchen, it was two slices of bacon left. O was going completely the fuck off. However, I expected it because Deron gave no fucks at all. His nickname was CROIX. In French, CROIX meant cross, and if he crossed some food at yo house, his ratchet ass was eating it. We got to the gas station. "Yo, I'm a go in and get me some gummy worms. You want something?"

"Nah mane. I'm good." O got out and went inside the joint while I sat in my car and waited for the pump attendant to come up to the car. After about two minutes, seeing how I got caught up playing a game on my phone, I looked around. Granted I was the only one at the pump right now, but where were these cats at? I didn't see anyone. Now, I had to get out and complain to the manager. His peoples weren't where they were supposed to be. Omarr was coming out the inside as I was walking towards it. "Yo where these fools at?"

"What fools?," he said, slurping whatever was in that big ass slurpee cup.

"The damn attendants."

"Hold on, hold on," O said, as I turned around. "Man, they changed that shit. You gotta pump ya own gas now."

"WHAT???!!!"

"Yeah man. Pump ya own gas."

"When did they change this shit?"

"Sometime this year." I couldn't believe this. I walked back to the pump and started to pump my own gas. I swear the more things change the more they stayed the same. "Yo man," O said through the open passenger side window. "Let's hit up Pine State. Ya boy hungry."

"Fuck it. And don't think I forgot about you owing me this." I looked at the screen at the pump. "$72.90. I need my shit."

"Aight damn man. Just get in the damn car." I finished up and we headed for Northeast Portland. It used to be the hood, but that gentrification shit was real. All the bruhs were now in Southeast, because they uprooted the shit outta my folks. It was crazy how this was occurring all throughout the nation. You see, this nation has never let any race outside the Caucasian race go past 13%. When the Latinos got to 16%, they got to sending out ICE and deporting as much as they could. It was literally black and brown versus them. We arrived at Pine State Biscuits. Wasn't no line, which was definitely a relief to say the least. We waltzed through the narrow North Alberta street til we hit the inside. "**TWO REGGIE DELUXE JOINTS MAN!!!**"

"Damn fool," I told Omarr. "Can you at least get to the counter first."

"What are you talking about fool? This my man's Doug. Sup Doug?"

"Waddup Omarr." They shook up.

"Something to drink?"

"Two sweet teas man."

"Aight. I'll get 'em to your table."

We walked back to the patio. Outside, it was a few people congregated together. In the back corner, however, was a light skinned cat sipping a tea by himself. He was damn near white with his Klay Thompson complexion. "Yo, let's go over here," Omarr said. "Who this dude?," I whispered to him. He either didn't hear me or he totally ignored me. "Yo wassup boy," O said to the dude, as they gave each other dap, with ol' boy just smiling, not saying a word. "Bruh. This my mans I was telling you about. Big Darnell. Darnell. This my little young gunner I done had under my wing. Tep." Me and homey shook hands.

"Tep? That's it?"

"Short for Imhotep man." I nodded my head. I knew the woke era was in effect, but I ain't know brothers was naming their kids after pharaohs and shit. "So who named you?," I asked him as we all sat down. "My mama from Kemet. Trust me man. I got enough black blood running through my veins. I know who I am." Things had gotten tense when I didn't try to have it that way. "Look man. I ain't mean to come off on you like that."

"Naw man. I get it. I'm damn near white. Don't look like I'm one of y'all. I know. I been fighting all my life with this. Thanks Doug." I looked up as he was bringing me and O our sweet teas. Soon as he left, Tep was back on it. "I was down in Birmingham once when I was a teenager. Let some fools rig me up. Damn near fought another brother. And why? Cause I didn't feel black enough? Nah man. Not anymore. That time of my life is over. I know who I am." I sipped my tea, just taking in everything this young dude just said. "Man, I swear. This world is ending man," I said, taking a sip of this fire ass tea.

"Why you say that?," O said.

"I'm pumping my own gas in Oregon, brothers wearing shorts with suits, and Bloods and GD's having babies together." O had a smirk on his face, squinted his eyes and his head went back. "Man what?," he told me. "I mean shit. None of this shit go together. Just watch. They getting prominent black men on sex charges. They gone get a sister next. Gotta destroy us all the way around."

"Yo Omarr. Ya boy wild mane. Get this muthafucka a Prozac."

"Hold on you lite bright, Klay Thompson complected muthafucka."

"Aight Aight y'all," O said, throwing both hands in the air. "We don't need any of this. Let's bring it back down. Discuss some shit like men. Now look, Darnell. You did your thang. I commend you. But I need to know that my man fifty grand gonna be willing to help my young partner here." I looked

125

over at this Pharaoh Monch ass dude with the grin you gave when you really didn't like someone. "Sure thing man." He knew what this look was cause the anger on his face said it all. "Tep. You good with that man?" That boy was looking dead at me, completely ignoring O. "Tep." Still nothing. "Tep?"

"Do you know why a black man has nine lives Darnell?" I ain't know what the hell this young dude was getting at. "Here you guys go. Two Reggie Deluxe sandwiches and one Reggie for you Tep." Doug dropped the food off and left, leaving us right back at square one. "Young dude what is you talking about?" Omarr wasn't paying us any attention at this point, as his mouth was literally engulfed in that sandwich. "I'll holla at you later man. Let's eat bruh." I shook my head and went to town. I forgot how good this shit was being gone for a year. Maybe it was a good thing. This had heart attack written all over it, and this was some shit that you didn't eat on a regular if you wanted to live a healthy life. We smashed up for the next thirty minutes, making small talk here and there. The tension from earlier was gone and it seemed like everything was back on one accord. Food would do that to you. Once we were done, all three of us got in my whip and headed towards downtown Portland to hit the office. I swear if felt good than a muthafucka to hit that bridge. Shit, if Portland didn't have anything else in the city, it damn sure had bridges. I got to the office building in this eclectic city and drove into the underground garage. Time had indeed shifted back to what I was once accustomed too. "Feel good don't it?"

"Man, you just don't know bruh," I answered to Omarr, as I stretched my arms outside the car, taking in the whiff of this great Pacific Northwest air. Tep wasn't saying much, as he was attached to his phone. "You still know the way?," Omarr asked me.

"Of course." We hit the elevator and it was on our way to the 35th floor. The elevator was so reflective of how our lives go at times. Up and down, up and down. Much like the elevator, we controlled what floor we arrived on or skipped. We had control. No one else, regardless of what some people say. It was amazing how you could think outside the box in something so simple as an elevator. I looked over at Omarr and Tep. They were both deep into their phones. I was more amazed that both of them had some sort of reception in here. The every so famous ring sounded and it was off and down the hall for us. I started to get into a business state of mind. Focused and direct. The irony about the G.O.O.D.S. office was the fact that unlike the rest of the office spaces in the building, the G.O.O.D.S. offices had tinted windows. One thing I respected about Omarr is that he didn't let too many people in his inner circle. As he would always say when I was around him. "You only give people a sneak peek. Never a full view." I got to the door first as they were not too far behind me. "Open up man. Your key still works." That was music to my ears. I shuffled through the keys in my pocket and found my gold striped card attached to my keyring. I set it in front of the scanner. With two flashing blue lights and a full illuminated green one, I heard the most magical click ever. We walked in. "**SURPRISE!!!**" I was in complete shock as Omarr shook the living hell out of my shoulders. The office was full of many of the same faces I left behind. The tables in the middle of the main space were full of food trays. I saw salt and pepper wings, black eyed peas and a gaggle of other shit, including fried okra that I was about to throw down on. "Damn man. Why you ain't tell me? I wouldn't have eaten them damn biscuits."

"You'll be aight. But, let's rap after you done saying your hello's and shit. I'll be in the office." Omarr walked off as one by one people came up to greet me. It was all a dream to me. This is where I saw my life take off. I spent a good five to seven minutes greeting folks and shooting the shit. I observed Tep in the far corner of the room, texting on his phone. I thought nothing major of it and went over to Omarr's office door. I knocked four times. "**COME IN!!!**," I heard him shout from the inside. I strolled on in, looking at the giant 70 inch that was sitting on the adjacent wall. Omarr had on an old replay of a Blazers game that always haunted him. It was that one where the Lakers came back in Game seven of the Western Conference Finals and Kobe threw that lob to Shaq that shook the whole arena. "Man, it's been 18 years bruh. You gotta let this shit go."

"Nah man. Nah. I can't. Ain't no way in hell you supposed to blow this shit. It's already a speck of bruhs in this town. You had a group of bruhs that had a chance to turn this place into crunk city. They simply turned it into slump city." He cut the television off as I sat down on the plush couch in front of his desk. Fam bam smiled at me and I returned it. He leaned back in that recliner of his, folding his hands. "How you feel man? Honestly."

"Man," I said scratching my head. "This shit man. It's been the hardest thing ever."

"I know man. I know."

"Man, when we agreed on this shit, I thought it would be the easiest shit ever. One year, 50 million. Easy day. But I'm starting to become something I'm not."

"But that's what the old man's purpose was the whole time bruh. I mean shit. Honestly. Look at every major figure on TV right now. You think that's them twenty-four seven? Hell nah man. That's something they show us for the cameras. When they on their own time, they finally can be who they are. That was the whole purpose man." He held up the packet that altered my entire life. "I made a copy," as he tossed it down in front of me on his desk. I grabbed it, opening it up and just skimmed through the pages. "You know I didn't use to believe that saying man. But, after this year, I learned it to be true. You live a lie for so long and eventually, you start to believe the shit." I was referring to the false prison record that was made up for me. The stories I was told to sell to those I encountered out in North Dakota. The fake shit about working for a mechanic. All I ever shared with them was the work of some clever writers here at the magazine. Not even my college experience was true, minus the football escapades. The fight. The fight never happened. That day I went in to talk with that athletic director, I knew who had made those calls to him. Telling him my story. The shit got me in. Now, I had to get out, because I was literally losing my mind without the interference of white people. "So, who this kid you were telling me about a while back man?"

"Oh Twon. Twon man. He a special case man. I've seen this little dude at his lowest. He in my ex-con class. Homey just turned 20 not too long ago. He working though. He working to get better. I'll give him that."

"And he staying with you right?"

"Yeah man. Yeah. He at the house right now, probably fuckin up all my shit. I ain't know that I was gonna get that close to him man. I gotta tell him the truth. I'll feel bad if I just pop up and disappear out of his life one day."

"Well. Big Dog," Omarr said stretching. "That's what you gone have to do. You just gotta figure out how it's gone play out. You literally got days now my guy. But, the old man left something here for you." Omarr reached underneath his huge desk and pulled out a silver briefcase, dropping it on the table and pushing it over to me. "All for you man. Your work. Not mines." I grabbed it from both sides and pulled it towards me slowly. I was acting like it was a bomb in it, knowing damn well it wasn't. If the old man was gonna kill anyone, it damn sure wouldn't have been Omarr. He loved this dude like his own son from the way Omarr talked about him. I opened up the briefcase and my eyes lit up. "The fuck," I said in a whisper, looking into something I never saw at any time in my life. "That's a full mil," Omarr said.

"I see mane I see." I was still in awe at the sight. I held a six-figure check for my own work before, but never saw a million in cash up close and personal. "That's the old man's thank you gift for lasting this long. He knew it wasn't gone be easy, so he figured he'd give you a little bonus to finish it out."

"Where he at man?"

"At his mansion. Surrounded by his folks. He ain't got much time left man. His address in there."

"Whatchu mean he ain't got much time?"

"Boy you don't remember shit huh? Like I said, he ain't got much time. He say he waiting for you. He ain't leaving this earth til he sees you. Don't ask me about some wacky ass spiritual shit, because I don't know. All I know is that he says he waiting for you."

"Aight man. Here. Hold this." I handed him back the briefcase. "What you giving it back to me for?," he asked, as I got up and walked towards the door. "Fool I ain't leaving yet. All that food out there. Oh, I'm gone smash."

"Dude. We just ate."

"Do you know the last time I had black eyed peas made by black people with some hard-fried wings and other black folks shit?" Omarr started laughing his ass off. "Aight greedy ass. Get to it."

"And fuck you," I said back jokingly, with a middle finger directed right at him. "The same amount of black folks in this other room is the same amount I done seen in North Dakota my whole time." Fam chucked the deuce cross his forehead as I went out of his office and to the table to smash. Forty-five minutes later, I came back in. That fool was still watching that game. I grabbed my briefcase and headed towards the elevator. I pressed the button, only to see that this thang was all the way down on the sixth floor. I hated waiting a long time for elevators, but it was what it was. "Mind if I roll with you?" I turned around after hearing that voice. It was Tep. "Nah man. Omarr gone have to give you a ride wherever you're going back too. I got some business to take care of."

"It's all good," he said. "I'm headed downstairs with you. I'll catch me an uber somewhere." I really didn't care what the young pup was gonna do, so I just shrugged my shoulders and waited patiently. The elevator came up and we both stepped in, taking us down, first to the lobby, where he exited without saying a word. Next, it was down to the parking garage to get to my whip. I was solo and walking through a somewhat lit garage, starting to think about that night at the club where I saw that creepy old man. I heard a noise in the distance and whipped my head around. I was low key paranoid. I had a milli in the briefcase and didn't know who might know. Plus, I didn't have a burner on me at the time, so I was fair game for anyone to try and crack off on me. I managed to make it to my whip, keeping my head on a swivel every step of the way. I laid the briefcase on the passenger seat and sat down myself, shutting my door behind me. I literally let out a sigh of relief and a couple of deep breaths as I once again came back down to reality. Before I started up the whip, I threw in a Mic Capes CD. He was a local cat from Portland who was flame. Of course, however, when you thought about rap music, your first thought wasn't Portland. I vibed to the beat for a minute, still reeling in the feeling of being back home. I pulled out of my spot and headed for the outside streets. From downtown, I was on my way to Southwest Hills. Out here, it was one of those spots where you had to have money to live. This, Lake No Negro as we called it and many more areas weren't too fond of us out here in the whitest city in America, but that's life. It was a quick 10-15 minute drive, and everyone hadn't gotten off of work yet, so I was pretty much in the clear downtown with all these weird ass one-way streets. I got to the district, ensuring that I remembered exactly where the house was from the address Omarr gave me. The last thing I wanted was to be roaming around a neighborhood like this and the police come and pop my ass for driving while black. I pulled up on a sprawling home which looked like it came straight out of the colonial era itself. In the driveway was parked two all black Phantom Rolls Royce. Pulling up in the Lac truck, it was almost the equivalent of pulling up in a Volkswagen. I exited out of the car, briefcase in hand. I observed my surroundings. I looked two homes down and noticed an elderly white man looking at me as if I wasn't supposed to be here. I mean he stopped watering his lawn and all. That was strange to me. All this money these people had. Ain't no way in hell I'd be outside watering my own grass. Then again, when you have the amount of money some people have, you do shit just to pass the time by. I rang the doorbell, which provided a softening tune that could just soothe your soul if you were having a bad day. The door then creaked open. A man in a suit opened up. "Hello sir. I'm here to see."

"He is waiting for you in his quarters." The butler or whoever this guy was held the door all the way open. I took two steps in and was simply amazed at the sight. I had seen some shit in my day, but never the shit that people in the literal 1% tax bracket had. Honestly, I didn't know if I was walking into Candyland's house from Django, or just a shit tight awesome mansion. I followed the butler up the winding staircase, still amazed at the chandelier that dangled from the top of the home. We made it to the top of the stairs to two huge wooden doors with art carvings in them. It looked like the highest quality of redwood and the sculptures of hieroglyphics were jaw dropping. That indeed was weird to say the least for an old white man to have. The man in the suit knocked on the door and poked his head inside. I patiently waited behind him. No words were said, until he stuck his head back out to me. "You may enter sir." He pushed the door open and I walked into a sprawling bedroom that was the size of some people's one bedroom apartment. "Mr. King. So happy to see you," the old man said, sitting in his plush chair off to the right of his Cali king. "Come take a seat," as he pointed his finger to the plush couch that was also sitting adjacent to his chair. "Nice artwork on the door sir. Didn't realize a man of your stature would be interested in African culture. No disrespect of course. Just odd to see."

"What you saw Mr. King, was the reincarnation of the tomb scriptures inside of the tomb of Ramses the Fourth, buried in the Valley of the Kings, in the city of Thebes."

"Imhotep?," I said, shocked as this was the last person I had expected to see. He had literally popped out the bathroom wiping his hands with paper towels, shocking the living shit out of me. "It damn sure ain't the President."

"Wait. I'm confused," said the old man. "You two have met before?"

"You can say that dad. Small world isn't it Mr. King?," Tep said, sitting down on the edge of the bed.

"Where did you meet my son?"

"Bumped into him at Clackamas dad. We were in the Oregon State store. Two random fans. Just started choppin' it up. Always kind of awe inspiring to know a random person isn't so random. Isn't that right Darnell?" I thought I could come up with a good lie on the spot. This muthafucka was an expert in that shit. "You right man. You right," as I let out a small chuckle. That laugh was an act because I was truly still confused as fuck. I finally sat down on the plush couch as the old man had directed me to do earlier. "Darnell, do you know why I chose you?" I looked at Imhotep, hands folded, just mean mugging me. "Who's that in the picture?," I asked him. "Oh, that woman. That's my wife. Her name is Bintanath. She's on travel. So, back to my original question." I paused for a good minute. "No," I answered. "Ok, so here's why. One, I don't have much time. Do I have a terminal illness? No. It's something I tell the people near and dear to me. People somehow draw closer to you when they think you have cancer, some life altering disease or something like that. Me, I truly believe that when you know your purpose is complete, that it's time to move on. Not necessarily in the physical, but in any aspect of the human mind. You know the poor and those who were considered lower class built some of the most extravagant structures that the modern-day man still can't figure out. My son, he's black. As far as I'm concerned. If he has one drop in him, he is what built history. I saw you for all the work you did. I read your stories. I studied you. I watched your every move. You have so many positives, but one thing you are weak at. Living a lie. You watched your parents do it as Marines. They came home and were happy go lucky for the crowds of people who thanked them for their service. But deep down inside, they were traumatized. Sent to accomplish an agenda and not an actual war. What they saw was bloodshed for a dollar. You didn't wanna be that, but you vouched for them all the time because they were your parents. Which you were supposed to do. But still, it was a lie. You knew the truth. Then, you escaped and went to college. You weren't a football player, but you told yourself you were because your whole life had been defined on the movements of someone else. So, you lived a lie and actually became good at that lie. So, it was me. I compiled the lies for you to live away from everything you knew. It was me. I know everything. I know about Twon." That's when my heart started beating a million miles an hour. This guy had really researched me to the core. "I want you to read this tonight in your living quarters." He threw a square envelope at me, which obviously contained a book. "Have a good day Darnell. And remember. No journey is complete until it is finished. You may exit now." I couldn't do anything but get up. I had been hit with such a blow that words were futile at this point. I exited this man's bedroom in a hasty retreat and scurried down the stairs. The butler, server, whoever in the good hell he was, was there to open the door. I stormed out to my car, upset to say the least. "**DARNELL!!!**," a voice bellowed out. I turned around, eyes a little misty because I was for once exposed in my life. Imhotep was running up to me.

"What you want man?"

"Look man. My father. He cool. He just got a way with words. Whatever going on back there where you at, just face your demons bro. Get that truth out and you'll see that everything is all for the better."

"What you know about trials? Huh? You sit in this phat ass house, with your silver spoon. Your rich ass daddy. With Egyptian shit that makes you think you black. I mean, you got some tint on your skin, but you don't know nothing about a struggle man. Fuck out my face." He backed up two steps and nodded his head up and down. "Oh, I get it. You see a big ass house, a white daddy and you think my life been all peaches and cream huh? Lemme guess. You saw more hood shit then me, right? No wait, lemme guess again. You got a helluva lot more melanin in your skin, so that makes you officially black. I'm a mixed breed so I can't speak on the ill wills, right? I don't know what the struggle is. I don't know what it's like to go to a school full of white kids in the burbs. You know, out there in Tualatin and shit. Being asked what are you every fucking day? All because I look almost white, but not quite. You know what it's like for police to see you and just for a minute think that we got us one? But then, they take a closer look and realize who your dad is. So instead of bashing your head in, they roll up and say how's your dad? Is everything going well with business? Shit like that. Never ask about ya mom. Cause her skin a little darker. Welcome to Oregon nigga."

"What you call me?," I asked him, as I balled my fist up. "Man, nigga please. I got just as much black in me, if not more than you. My mama's ancestors, who are black, built all the shit that these muthafuckas still can't figure out today. So, don't you dare sit here and try to question my blackness because of my complexion or how I grew up. My struggle was not being around my kind, therefore I had to fight for my kind.

And it's a fucking shame that I spent my whole life fighting to show that I'm black to a bunch of uppity ass white folks. Now, I gotta fight another **NIGGA**, just to show him that we bred the same." Now, he was in my face. I wanted to lowkey punch this kid, but something was indeed holding me back. "I had to fight just to prove my worth whenever I got around my kind. You ever bomb a house? Simple question."

"No," I responded in a low, pissed off tone. "I have. I did that shit. Twelve, thirteen, I can't fucking remember, but someone died. I gotta body on my resume that I ain't proud of, all in the name of fuck my oppressor. I know who I am. So, if you wanna stand and judge because you don't understand, then that's fine. But my suggestion is that you find yourself and who the hell you are. I know you a God. We all Gods. But, the problem with yo ignat ass is that you too proud to see it inside yourself muthafucka." And with those words and his finger in my chest, my right hand connected with his jaw faster than Floyd Mayweather. He dropped to the ground and just looked up at me, holding his mouth. He slowly rose up, putting his hand to his mouth to feel the blood that was trickling from his lip. He was now standing in front of me still rubbing his lip. I myself was still ready to fight. "Now you see that same anger and aggression you just had? Use that going forward with finding yourself." He said that in a low tone that took me someplace out of body. "I'll be seeing you soon. Real soon." He turned around and walked back to the house. I watched his every step until he was out of sight. I don't know what in the good hell had gotten into me, but I had definitely just had an experience that I myself couldn't even explain. I went back into my car and just sat there for a minute, trying to recollect myself. I pulled off about five minutes later and headed towards my condo which was 30 minutes outside the city in Tualatin. I was gonna head straight home, but I diverted to 205 South and decided to head to Clackamas. It was a mall out here. I honestly don't know why I didn't go straight home, but sometimes a walk around the mall could clear ya head up. Once I got there, it was the same as usual. Nothing had changed since I had bounced over a year ago. Same ol' stores, same ol' vibe. Portland was just weird like that per say. I never felt threatened up here like I did in Miami. Just for clarification, I wasn't saying that stuff didn't happen up here, because it did. If you asked me, this was the place where all the brothers escaping their troubles in Cali came, with some added from Chicago. Shit popped off, but it wasn't nowhere near like it was in Miami. There wasn't a high chance that you were gonna see Rip City on the First 48. I walked in the mall and was immediately drawn to the Barnes and Nobles book store. Maybe it was the old man giving me a book to read. I had no idea. I did know however that reading and writing was a major key in the development of an individual. I made sure to always add some new lit to my collection. It was hard being in North Dakota keeping up with the book game, especially living the way I was living. But, for a moment, if only for a moment, I felt normal again. I scanned through the black book section. I had read enough of the rich dad, poor dad's, or any other entrepreneur books. I needed to delve back into my roots. Scanning through the numerous titles, my eyes never caught anything that pulled me and said take me home. I spent about an hour just combing through books, reading snippets of multiple joints in this one section. Then, after I had my fill, I simply exited the same way I entered. It took me 15 minutes to get to my place. It was crazy. I hadn't seen my crib in a year. I know Omarr and a few of the people from the mag were taking care of it, but I didn't fully trust folks when it came to my property. I scanned the digitized key along my door. The click was music to my ears. High security was something I relished ever since I had come into some money. I walked in and too my surprise, my place was cleaner than when I stayed here full time. My 70 inch was still there, clean as a whistle. The numerous art pics I had above my kitchen table were still standing the test of time. I walked down the hall to my master bedroom. On the way there, I relished in the poster sized pictures I had blown up of me and numerous celebrities I met throughout the years. My career had taken me far. It was crazy. One minute, you were calling and emailing everyone in their mama to try and get an interview with a high profile. The next thing you know, you hit a few events, make a few connections, and now those same celebrities were sending you formal invites to their functions. No more hoping to get in the game. You were in the game, and you became a master at playing it. I got to the bedroom and dropped my bags. "Oh, mama I have missed you so damn much." I said that out loud, as I literally jumped on my king size back first and just lie there for a good minute or two. It was good to be back. A crib fitting of Coronado, California in the suburbs of Portland. After my reacquaintance, I got off the bed and reached for the package the old man gave me that was now sitting on the floor.

I went back to the bed, tearing it open, wondering what book this guy had given me. The Power of Broke by Daymond John. The Seven Habits of Highly Effective People by Stephen Covey. I mean, a man worth hundreds of millions of dollars damn sure wasn't gonna give you a "Cooking with Weed" book by Caujuan Mayo, even though this state was known to burn the leaf at an alarming rate. I pulled the book from the package and was confused to say the least. The book had no title. It was literally a blank cover. I turned it around to the back. The same thing. Once I opened it up, I was even more confused. The book was written in a language that I had no clue what it was. I tossed the book down next to me, wondering what in the good hell was the old man trying to prove with this. Then, my spirit once again tugged at me and I picked it back up. I did a quick flip through all the pages. After the second flip through, I still couldn't find any part that was written in English. The only thing that I could make out were some of the drawings. Then, it hit me. I ran over to my stand-alone computer. My dumb ass spent 15 seconds moving the mouse around, not even thinking that I didn't even cut the bitch on. It would be a minute before it loaded up, so I took the time to go and unpack my two bags and get everything organized as much as possible. After that fiasco turned into half an hour, I went back to the computer with a glass of filtered water from the PUR that was attached to my faucet. Crazy thing is that these fools made sure the lights stayed on, the house stayed clean, but no food was anywhere in this thang. My refrigerator was bare as a baboon's ass. The screen loaded up and it was on to google, the modern-day replacement for education since people were too lazy to pick up a book. I googled Egyptian wall paintings and tried to find ones that matched some of the joints that I was seeing in this book. Finally, after ten minutes of surfing the web, I found one. I glanced between the screen and the book to make sure it was a match. It was. From what I was getting, it was Osiris, and he was casting his judgement on the dead to enter the afterlife. What was it with these people and all this Egyptian mumbo jumbo? Son named Imhotep. Mama named whatever the fuck. Dog probably named Amun Ra. Shit was wild. I was too lazy and not giving a flying fuck to look up anything else on this subject for the time being. I found the info I was looking for and I went right back to my bedroom, to catch me a good two to three-hour nap. It felt good to sleep in your own bed, even if it was for a limited time.

———————————

I heard my doorbell ringing constantly. It wasn't too many people who knew I was home, so the shit was disturbing to say the least. I figured that everyone I knew would had saw me at the office. But again, this wasn't where black folks lived typically. Up here, it was somewhat of a pass to be at someone's door without calling first. I didn't think much of it. Probably someone who missed me while I was downtown. I raised up and stretched on the edge of the bed. The doorbell rang again. "**HOLD ON!!!**," I yelled out. I got up, slid my feet into my house shoes and started to walk towards the front door. Luckily, the days of hitting my foot or ankle on that exposed piece of iron were over. When you had money, your bed was actually high quality and you didn't have those problems. I got to the door, rubbing my eyes one more gin when the doorbell rang again. "**OK. *** DAMN!!!**" I opened up the door. "Fuck on the floor man." That's all I heard, as I felt a hand around my neck and saw a gun in my face. "One move. I swear for Christ one move and you gone meet Him personally." I didn't know what was going on, rather I did, but I was still somewhat delusional. Here I was looking up at the barrel of a gun, while I heard other footsteps in the house, with someone rustling through my belongings. "Turn over," this guy told me through his orange bandana. I obliged with the quickness, trying not to give these guys any reason to take my life. "We ain't find it man," someone said from the hallway. "Get yo ass up," I was told, as I was snatched up by my t-shirt and tossed over to the couch. I was fucked up. The gun was still pointed at me. There were three gentlemen, all in orange bandanas. "So where is it?," the young brother with the gun asked me.

"What are you talking about?"

"**NIGGA WHERE THE FUCKING PACKS AT???!!!**" He then ran up on me and put the gun directly flush with my forehead. "Bruh. I God honest don't know what in the good hell you are talking about." The next thing I felt was the smack of the gun against the side of my head. "**GET THE FUCK UP!!!**" I was still groveling on the floor, holding the side of my head. I looked at my hand and it was covered in blood. I pulled myself back on the couch in so much pain. My head was literally gushing blood. "I'm gone ask you one more time. Where are the fucking packs?" Through blurred vision, I heard him cock the hammer back. "I told you," I said, struggling to see. "I God honestly don't know what you are talking about."

"Man blast this nigga," one of the other guys said. I was still dazed and confused, but the young brother with the gun pulled off the bandana on his face. "Imhotep," I whispered. No response. The gun went off and I felt the bullet hit me square in my right cheek. "**OH SHIT!!!**," I yelled, falling out my bed and smacking face first onto the floor. "Ahh shit," I said, bent over on my knees, holding my face. This shit hurt, not to mention that my phone was steady buzzing. I removed my hand and saw that it had blood on it. "**FUCK!!!**" I pulled myself up, back on my bed with my free left hand and reached for the phone. "Hello?"

"Man, why in the good hell you sound like you just finished jacking off?"

"Man, who this man?"

"This Omarr man. What the hell wrong with you?"

"Man, I had a dream someone broke in and shot me. Then, I fell out the bed, and I feel a gash above my eye."

"Damn bruh. Welcome home gotta whole new meaning now. Yo, you get them packs?"

"Man, what is you talking about?"

"Man, I sent you some packs of DVD's, new mags dropping, all that. Should've been at yo house already. I specifically had it scheduled for delivery today. If you ain't got them shits man, I gotta call these people."

Then, the doorbell rang. "Man, the doorbell ringing."

"That must be it man. Let me know how you dig the joints."

"Aight man. Gone."

"Later." I straggled over to the bathroom before anything. I looked in the mirror. I had a small cut above my right eye. It wasn't deep enough for stitches, but it damn sure left a mark. I had a fucking headache. The doorbell rang once more and I waltzed on over to the door with a rag on my eye. I opened the door.

"Darnell?"

"That be me. And this must be from Omarr."

"Yep, Sign here." I couldn't write for shit with my left hand, but I managed to scribble some trash truck juice on the electronic device he was holding. "Thanks. Have a good day." He could kiss my hairy black ass with the good day mess. I brought the box in and dropped it on the living room couch. I went to wash my hands and my wound, slapping one of those big ass band aids over it. I came back and cracked open the box, still in a bad mood. I looked inside and my mans had really put in work over the last year with the mag. I flipped through a couple of the 2017 issues and the shit was on point. While reading through the September 2017 issue, I saw one of my articles that I had written. I know I had a lot of content, but this was one story that I wasn't sure about. However, seeing that it was the five-star article of the month, I was truly humbled.

When Service meets Triumph

"Being challenged in life is inevitable, being defeated is optional." These words were spoken by Roger Crawford, who suffered from Ectrodactylism, yet became the first Division I player to compete in a major college sport(tennis) with a known disability. In life, upon graduating from high school, I was looking for a challenge that would allow me to grow as a human, but also mold me into a man. The challenge was discovered when I enlisted in the United States Navy. I managed to make it five years. In those five years, however, I faced some serious setbacks that were a result of my lapses in judgements. In 2015, I was charged and found guilty of violating the UCMJ under articles 97 and 102, losing rank in the process. In that time of restriction to the ship, I had time to step back and ask myself. What do I truly want in life? Well, the first thing I wanted was to make peace with my situation. I accepted my actions, consequences and decided from that point forward, I would become the change that many wanted to see. Others saw my potential, and I finally took a look at it myself. I gave it everything I could. I once again made third class petty officer, and later second class. The most amazing moment during this time was when I was trying to implore core values into other sailors that I had once taken for granted. They say a real man learns from his mistakes and tries to help others avoid them. It was at that point where I realized the molding of a man had indeed occurred. In my pursuit of becoming a Surface Warrior Officer, I looked to impact my shipmates and lead them to the best of my abilities. With my prior enlisted background, I knew the challenges that today's sailors face and it only enhances my leadership abilities by making me better at what I do. I was 100% ready to elevate to this position and take on any, and all responsibility. The Seaman to Admiral program offered me a motivated, dedicated and fully committed sailor like myself a once in a lifetime chance to receive a bachelor's degree, and further develop my capacity to become a United States Naval Officer. But then, I had a change of heart. I was young, motivated, but had to ask myself. Is this what I really wanted to do in life? I was a fashion guru and stayed laced in the highest quality. And one day, I responded to an open casting call for a local television show. I showed up in a steel grey suit, and that was all she wrote. Now, you see me in every magazine, television show, movie, all dappered down and making my moves. And to think. All of this started by getting in trouble when I was serving in the United States Navy. Remember, as the great college coach Jimmy Valvano once asked as he faced death from cancer. "How do you go from where you are to where you want to be? And I think you have to have enthusiasm for life. You have to have a dream, a goal. And you have to be willing to work for it." Indeed, I truly believe I have.

I didn't know the power of writing until I wrote that article on an veteran. I had actually written that a while back. 2015 to be exact. I thought it wasn't worthy of writing, but Omarr was persistent for me to turn it in and let it not rot on a hard drive. I shot it too him and told him to not print that shit in edition. To my luck, some military members got a hold of that article and a whole new audience was gained. America had a knack of loving the success stories of former service members. That was the article that skyrocketed my career and had me inking consistent six figure deals. I spent the next hour or so combing through DVDs full of interviews with A listers that the squad had conducted from Portland to Vegas to Hollywood and everywhere else you could imagine. I had really missed out on a lot and I was starting to kick myself in the ass. However, I had a bigger purpose to achieve. Ironically, I would achieve that truth through lying. My phone began to ring and I saw it was Twon. I stopped the DVD where Omarr was going ape shit crazy at the Super Bowl in Minneapolis when the Eagles beat Suge Brady, Bill Pacalypse now and Death Row Records. "What's up Twon?" There was silence on the other end, but I could hear emergency vehicles in the background. "Twon? What's going on?" My voice was cool, calm and collective. I didn't wanna jump to any conclusions just yet. "Umm. OG. I don't know how to tell you this. I burnt your place up."

"What do you mean you burnt my place up?" My attention was now locked in as I got up from the couch and walked outside. "Well. Umm. I tried frying some chicken. I put too much grease in the skillet and it overflowed into the fire. I didn't know what to do so I ran." At this point, the devil was slowly creeping up in my soul as I wanted to lash out at this kid. "Did you burn the building up or just my place?"

"Oh, that's the good thing OG. The fire department got here just in time to contain the fire to just your place. No other units were affected. Good right?" How in the good fuck do you even come to say the words good right when you burn up somebody crib? I didn't know if I wanted to kill this kid by chokehold or bury him on one of the reservations out there.

148

Then, reality hit. "You know what Twon. Don't worry. You gotta place to stay tonight?"

"**HUH!!!** I just burned your house down OG. You ain't mad?"

"Oh, I'm mad. Trust me. I'm mad. But, I need to know if you got a roof to sleep under tonight."

"I mean my mom's here because I called her."

"Then cool. Assist the investigators, chill with ya mom, keep grinding and I'll be back within the week alright?"

"You sure you not mad OG?" I paused for ten seconds. I wanted to make sure the next words that came out of my mouth would resonate with his soul. "They can renovate another apartment. They can't renovate and reincarnate another you. I'll holla." I hung up the phone and plopped back down on the couch. I wish I could've burned up my damn self. I spent the rest of the evening flipping through the channels. By eight o'clock, a brother was hungry again, so I got up and headed to B Dubs for a twenty piece. Life was nuts at times to say the least.

Three days had passed and I had seemed to settle back into my surroundings. I had two days left here to figure out how I was gonna face my demons that awaited me back in North Dakota. In the meantime, I took the time to re do so much. I got a new furniture set for the crib. I scheduled a complete renovation to where I would get new wood tile and carpet within the next two weeks. Today, though, I had to take care of some other business which would see me drive three hours north to Bellevue, Washington. What the hell was up here you ask? Money. I learned in my time that money was everywhere.

An entrepreneur and a hustler were two different entities. A hustler would do a deal with a Klan member to make some money. An entrepreneur would do deals that fed him for a lifetime, and today was that day. I spent about five hours total up there, not including the three hour drive it took me to get there. I blazed back and hit Portland city limits around eight at night. I was dead tired. Luckily, Omarr called a brother on the road and kept me upbeat. I got home and just chucked the deuce to anything electronically, minus the lights. I put the phone on the table, the television stayed off and I could just kick back in peace. As I was sitting, I looked over towards my mailbox slot. There was a solo envelope. It was strange as hell, cause even though O and the crew took care of my place, my mailing address had been forwarded to where I was at. I didn't have anything coming here. Not just yet. I debated on getting up and getting that shit. Eventually, fuck it was the word that my mind gave me, and I got up and got it. There was no return address, so this had been delivered by someone personally. I put one finger under the slit and ripped it open. My eyes lit up like the Fourth of July. "Half a mill. Man, who in the hell?" I took my eyes off the numbers and read the company. "G.O.O.D.S. magazine. Nah. Ain't no way." I called O up and tried to hash this out. "A man. I ain't mad, but you sent me a check for half a mill?. What's this for?"

"Man, I ain't sent you shit," he said, obviously in the whip driving from the way his voice was coming thru the phone, with the wind giving a slight howl in the background. "Bruh. I swear on my mama I just opened an envelope that was delivered to the house. It says the company cut it." "Hold on man. Lemme pull over." Things got silent as Omarr pulled over. A few minutes passed and he then broke his silence. "Bruh, I just checked the account. Ain't nothing missing. So, whatever you got, it ain't from us."

"You check the old man?"

"He doesn't work for us."

"Good point."

"Well man, I dunno, but don't break that shit. Ain't tryna get flagged you know."

"Fosho man. I got you."

"Gone." Shit was weird to say the least, but I put it back in the envelope and kept it under lock and key. Pretty sure that I would get an explanation on this shit sooner than later. I waltzed into my bedroom and started to pack up. I only had one day left and I wanted to have my shit together, and not wait until the last minute. Tomorrow, I had a few last errands to run. Actually, those errands were custom suits. 50 to be exact. I had to keep my dress game up to the T. That's how my daddy was, and the apple didn't fall to far from the tree. I had a custom tailor over in Beaverton, out there by the Nike factory. It wasn't too many brothers up here who owned suit stores, so I definitely had to take advantage. I walked in cool, calm and collective that evening as I saw my man Johnny Black straightening out the shoe collection. "**JOHNNY!!!**" He snapped his head around and a huge grin came across his face. "Man, I thought beef steak had a ton of fat on it. Boy you come in here looking fat free and organic my nigga, **COMMERE!!!**" I dapped my fam bam up. "Shit man long time no see."

"I know man I know. I heard about the old man and the tasking he gave you. 50 M's my G. 50 M's," he said, punching my chest.

"Yeah mane yeah. A man. Need some shit."

"C'mon on over to the wall. Show you what we got in." We walked into a concealed door which led into a room which he called The Crackhouse. "Now, first off. Hold on." Johnny pulled his phone out his pocket.

"OH SHIT NIGGA!!!"

"What's crackin'?"

"LEBRON COMING HOME FOOL!!!"

"Man, what you talking about? He is home." That's when he flashed the phone in front of my face.

"Damn. Four years, one fifty-four."

"Can you say championship boy?"

"You think he really getting past the Dubs?" My mans looked down at his phone again. **"DAMN AND WE JUST GOT EAR BLOWER LANCE!!! YO!!! LARRY HOOVER LANCE!!! I DONT GIVE A FUCK!!!** He can blow in any nigga ear he wants to now. He on the winning squad."

"Man, I thought you was Trailblazers all the way."

"Man look here. Fuck them niggas. The King is home at my original franchise. Now what you want? The camel hair joints. Italian wool. Or here. I got the Lebron special. Gold suit, made out of Malaysian cotton." I had to laugh at that one. That one was funny to say the least.

"Naw man. I need a big order."

"Like how big?"

"50 suits."

"**50 SUITS NIGGA!!!** Look here man. I'm a tailor, not a magician."

"Naw naw bruh. Here." I handed him the measurements on a sheet of paper. Hook me up with what I need. You choose the colors. I know you got everything I need." Fam bam looked over the list.

"Gimme a month man."

"Coolio." I dapped fam up and turned around to walk out. "A man. Hold up." I turned around, back in the main part of the store.

"Waddup man?"

"Come here man. Follow me." I gave him a strange look because I was trying to figure out where in the good hell else this dude was trying to take me. I walked back in the room. "A shut the door behind you." Now things had gotten really weird. I slowly shut the door, skeptical of what was upcoming. "Where we going?"

"Just come on man. Watch man. Got something to show you." We walked over to a safe in the wall. Johnny then started to enter a combination. A click followed and a wall began to slide out. He looked at me. "Man, what the fuck is this? Kingsman black edition." He laughed. "Just follow me man." We headed down a lit staircase. There were at least twenty stairs. This shit was nuts. We got all the way down to a door. "You ready?"

"Man, you done brought me down here. Might as well show me." He knocked three times. The door opened to a big, burly, bald headed black brother. He stood at least 6'7. This dude had to be at the minimum 340. "Who this?," he asked, pointing at me.

"Man don't question me Duke. I pay you, don't I?"

"Who this?," he asked again.

"Man, if you don't get yo big brick-built ass out the way?"

"I'll kick yo little pancake stacked high ass up and down this staircase Johnny boy." I was sitting here confused not knowing if these dudes were playing or had they gotten serious. They both let out laughter. "C'mon in nigga." I followed into the 6x9 space as big man shut the first door. He then proceeded to open the second door. That's when my eyes got big. Migos was blaring through the speakers as I literally was stuck in a trance. "Welcome to the show homeboy. Here. Have a cigar." Johnny passed me back an authentic Cuban. "C'mon man. Lemme show you around." I followed my man's as this was where the casino met the club. It looked like some shit out of Superfly. I saw man, man, woman, woman, woman, woman. I mean, it literally repeated itself. It was so much ass in here that I barely could contain myself. Continuing to walk through, I saw bruhs in sharp suits at crap tables. Three women were dancing on top of platforms. The bar area was oh my God to say the least. It at least stretched eight feet across and had the liquor stock of seven planets. Johnny tapped me on my chest. "Come to my office man." I wasn't questioning him on this one. I just followed, locking eyes with a few people. This was an amazing sight if I ever had saw one. "Shut the door behind you," he told me. I closed the door to this simple, yet plush office. The desk was made out of solid redwood. The couch that I plopped my ass on was softer than goose feathers.

He kicked his feet up on his desk. Not to mention that the door to his office was all powerful because I heard no music or anything. Johnny lit up a cigar and inhaled. The exhale was something straight out of a gangster flick. "Here man. Gimme yearns." I tossed it to him and he cut it, handing it back to me. "Lean over man." I got up and leaned over his desk, as he flickered the gold plated lighter. I took a few puffs and there she went. The shit was smooth. "By the way. This real gold. I know you probably think this was gold plated or some shit. Only thing fake round here is some of those titties in the next room. "Man, how did you get all this?"

"Cause you my mans. Just cause you my mans. I know you 1000 and shit won't leave this room. I operate on the black market. All that material upstairs, I got my connects from overseas. Black market special. Oh, the store is legit. The business is legit. How I get my product? That's another story. Now, how I don't get caught? Mighty glad you asked that, even though you didn't. Everyone of importance comes through that room. Police, the feds, fire department officials, politicians. Hell, I've even had a few high dignitaries come through here from overseas. See everyone plays the game, but only a few play it to the highest degree. Take the NBA for instance. You got Jordan, Lebron, Kobe, Bill. Some of the greatest brothers you know who killed it at their peak. They play the game. The second-tier guys. Third tier. Bench scrubs who comes in at the end. Yeah, they play, but they don't master it. You got those who get the check. Then, you have those who orchestrate the residual. That's me. And to get that, you have to have all hands-on deck, as they say in the Navy. Now,

155

at the same time, you gotta move people out the way. Play chess, not checkers. You remember them two niggas who L.A. traded to Cleveland right?"

"Clarkson and Nance."

"Yeah. Get them niggas out of there to free up some money so the King could come in and do his thang. That's called chess nigga. Rookies play checkers. Masters yell checkmate. Is it clear?" I puffed the cigar one time. "Crystal my dude."

"My nigga. Well look. I got champagne in here if you wanna chill and talk. I know its ya last night, so it's on you if you got the time. Go out, have a little fun on the tables if you wanna. Just do ya thang. I'll be here man," Johnny said, pouring up a glass of some unknown shit that looked amazing as it flowed out. "Man, I'll stay in here man. Let's catch up. I'm out in the early afternoon." He poured up another glass and handed it to me. "To 50 million," he said. I gave him a crazy look as I kept this glass in the air. "Oh, don't look at me like that nigga. I know. Trust me, I know. You had money. Now, you got wealth. Remember what I do. You think it ain't niggas in there who don't know what your bout to get? Remember. You wanna know what goes down? Follow the path of the wealthy white man. It never fails." There was a knock at the door. Johnny looked over at the camera screens as did I. I saw three men in black suits, with one containing a briefcase. Fam pressed a buzzer which in turn clicked the door open. The three men entered, said no words and just put the briefcase on the desk. "Thank you, gentlemen." They turned around and exited, simply not saying a word. Johnny hit the four latches on the case and opened it up, smoke billowing from his cigar. An evil laugh bellowed from him as he put his cigar down. "Congrats my nigga. Yo shit is officially over." He turned the briefcase around. My eyes got wide.

"Man how the fuck bruh?"

"What did I just tell you brother? Follow the wealthy white man and everything is over with." In it was the pics of my burned down apartment, a bundle of money and a Cuban. "Now you think the young gunna at yo crib actually set a grease fire? Well, actually he did. However, I told you. We know how to maneuver when you follow the wealthy white man. At some point, we knew the young brother had to cook. He couldn't cook no oxtails, greens, macaroni, shit like that. Hell, the boy could barely even boil water. So, that left two things. Either Ramen Noodles, or he was gone try to prove to himself that he could be self-sustained. And how do most youngins do that?"

"By frying some shit."

"See, you learning and you know. Frying is the simplest shit ever. Drop some shit in grease and let it float when it's done. One day, when he was out, those folks went in your apartment. Jerry rigged the stove. The plan was to burn the place all along. So even if he had of fried some catfish, chicken or whatever properly, at some point when he cut the stove on, it was gonna go up in smoke. Didn't want him to die. That's why we only allowed for it to happen when the stove was on. We knew he would get the hell outta there. Now, insurance money comes back to who, I ain't gone say. One of my loyal ones, a fire chief out there, him and his people got some hefty sums. All in the name of keeping the money, and never disclosing the money trail. What jigsaw say. If you good at anticipating the human mind, it leaves nothing to chance. That check from the university. We knew you would give it to Twon. Shit you really think that athletic director was looking you up on his computer when you were in that office? Naw nigga. He was reporting back. We knew you'd perform to the T. We know you. Now, you simply being rewarded. Now, toast up nigga." I wasn't gone question shit else. I simply tapped glasses with my mans and took a good swig of the drink. I don't know what this shit was, but since it came in a black bottle, I was gonna personally call it the black beauty, cause the shit went down beautifully.

The next day, eleven o'clock had come around too fast. I spent the night in a hot tub with six women, Johnny B. and a brother who stayed out in Macau, China. Shit was wild to say the least. Not making it back to the crib until four in the morning wasn't the business, and I really didn't get any sleep. However, I really couldn't complain after last night. The flight into Fargo was smooth and relaxing to say the least. I was in a navy-blue checkerboard suit, with alternating light orange and brown pinstripes. Baby blue shirt, tan penny loafers and a skinny navy-blue tie. I walked through the airport admiring the stares of the people, fully awake from the sleep I caught on the plane. White folks in this part of the country weren't accustomed to a sharp looking black man around these parts. The huge difference on this return is that I didn't have any luggage with me. My goal was to get in and get out. I went to the rental car joint and got me a Lexus with tint all the way around. It was summer, warm out and I knew exactly where Twon was. I knew exactly how I was gonna break things down to him. My people had gotten my mind right. I dipped up out the airport. How good was I feeling? I stopped at McDonald's and got me an angus burger. That may not seem like something big, but who in the good hell ate McDonald's still? Well, let me rephrase that. What normal, competent, functioning human being ate that shit? I cruised the streets headed to the facility where we met up at for our meetings. I knew this was Twon's safe haven when he wasn't at the house. He usually came up to the center by himself and worked on his reading and writing skills. And truthfully, that was some of the best shit that I could actually admire. The stats on literacy across America was appalling. 8,000 quit high school on a daily. 66% of eighth graders couldn't read at that grade level, and the same amount of youth living in poverty didn't have books in the home. And when they didn't have books in the home, as a kid living in the slums, they were more prone to get their education from the streets, and we didn't need any more of that shit. I pulled up to the center and saw the door wide open. Cars were in the parking lot, so business was in operation as usual. As I got out and straightened up my suit, wiping myself down, I saw Twon coming out the door, book in hand. "**YOUNG GUNNA!!!**" He looked over. "**OG!!!**" He came down the steps and then jogged it over to me. "Yo, what's up? Like, for real. What's up? Man, you look like you just jumped out a casket man. Like you a dead man who came back for a purpose." All I could do was laugh. "Is this your Lexus too?"

"Naw man. That's just a rental." He looked between the car and myself.

"Yo, what the hell was you doing up there in Portland?"

"I gotta tell you something Twon."

"What's that?"

"Hold on." My text message notification went off. "Let him down easy." It was Johnny B. It was like everyone was watching. So, as how I have always been, I went against the grain. "Aight look man," as I placed my phone back in my pocket. "Here's the end all to end all. I was a businessman back in Portland before I came out here. Truth be told, I only came out here to fulfill an obligation. I survive a year, living as a poor man, then I inherit 50 million dollars. That's life changing money Twon. That's the truth. That's the best way I can put it." I looked at him through my shades. He started to laugh. "Nah man. Nah. So hold on. You telling me. You came out here to live as a poor man for a year. Inherit some money and then bounce?"

"Yeah." He laughed again.

"That's a good one OG. I dunno know who put you up to this, but man that's a good story. Look, nice suit, wherever you got it from. You coming through the meeting tonight? I'm reading this book right here that I wanna rap about." He handed it to me. It was a joint called Black Lies Matter, with the word Lives crossed out. "Nice. By that brother Taleeb Starkes. Great damn author. He got another joint called the Un-Civil War that I've read. But what are you trying to imply?"

"Man nothing. Just wanna rap about the book with y'all old heads." I felt this young brother knew something that

160

I didn't. I wasn't surprised, seeing how many people knew about my situation. "Look here mane," I said, reaching in my pocket. "Here." I went through a wad of cash and pulled out $1000 in hundreds. I handed it to him and the look on his face was one of shock. "I told you. This ain't my life. I don't care about none of this shit. You a cool kid man. You really are. But you on ya own now. Take that bread. Help ya moms out. Buy yourself some gear. I don't give a shit. I simply came back here to tell you that I'm gone man." He backed up two steps. "Oh, I get it. Oh, so none of your life was what you said it was huh? You come here and make a mockery of the struggle. Do that, while back home ya rich ass got money stashed away for eons. Let me tell you something. I may be not even legal to drink, but I know about pain. You think niggas in Soundview act poor? You think niggas in Southside Chicago is acting? Opa Locka niggas in Miami acting? **THIS IS LIFE FOR US!!!** This place here. This ain't shit. But guess what. I ain't heard one fucking gunshot since I been here. I ain't seen a dead body, nor a drug deal, none of that. Nigga this is paradise. And the difference is that I don't act. I lived it. I've been robbed as a six-year-old by older niggas. I got a juvie record. I had no choice but to fly straight and narrow. But one thing I never did. I never lived a lie. So, take your fucking money and your life."

He threw the money at me and I watched it bounce off my chest. I thought about Big Boi in the movie ATL when he pulled out the gun after T.I. threw the money at him. I didn't have a pistol on me, but still, I wanted to slap the living daylights out of this little dude. "Twon?"

"**FUCK YOU OLD NIGGA!!!**," he shouted as he walked away towards the street. I shook my head. Young buck would just have to live with it. I mean, time heals all right? Shit happens and you get over it. I picked my money up from off the ground. Don't care how rich I was. I wasn't gonna just let a grand sit on the concrete. I took one look at the building that I would never step foot in again, chucked a deuce and drove off to the downtown hotel where I would be laying at for the night. Indeed, my work was done, and now I could return to the life that I had worked so hard to obtain.

THE END ALL TO END ALL

DEAR TWON. By the time you read this, I will have been long departed from this earth. You will have inherited a substantial amount of money that I left for you in my will. However, I feel you need to know the truth. Everything that I told you, how I felt about you and the struggle. It was real. I always empathize with those who didn't have the chances that I had growing up. The military always took care of its families. The struggle I endured was only real to an extent. The jail time never happened. I never worked at the university truly. I was at a simple junior college, helping out athletes, passing the time by. I only threw a big-time school name on it because I knew it would peak and keep your interest in obtaining a higher degree to not just education, but to life in general. The jail record thing. That was doctored up for me. Even the story of me in the courtroom spitting some Pac to the judge. All that shit was falsified. Cleavon, he was in on it the whole time I found out. Collecting checks for his work. His record holds true. Vice Lord, pimpin', gangbangin' in Chi City. Mines, however, did not. But, we knew it would get you to change. I know you saw that Mr. Cleavon died. Sad ain't it. People were sending me pics from the wake. Only nigga I know who would be buried in a whole rainbow of colors and look good. Any who. Montana, I played there. I actually once did get spat on and I dropped his fat white ass. They ain't lock me up though. Gotta remember that the black athlete is too valuable to their money scheme up there. Had I been at a Florida, LSU or a school like that, I probably would have been booted off the team and arrested. But, we talking Montana here, lol. Look up the stats man. In Missoula, where the college is at, it's about 365 of us. One for each day of the damn year. And you can chalk up about 104 of us inside the actual university due to sports. So, in actuality, it's under 265 full time. Miami, I lived it. Portland, I lived it. That's true. Then, one night, I met a man. I still don't know who he was, or where he came from. He asked me. What good is it for a man to gain the entire world and lose his soul in the process? Then, he gave me a quarter. Well, today, I lost my soul so that you could gain the entire world. At 8:57 p.m., on a Monday night, my world came to an end and your world had just begun. I thought about the best way to go out. So, here's what really happened. I sat on the corner of my couch. I pulled the redwood living room table that I purchased a little closer to me. I was so excited to see myself actually get that table. I drank a lethal dose of some mixed-up chemicals. You'll never know what they were. Just know that I researched it to the T. However, I knew that they would cause cardiac arrest and internal hemorrhage. I sat on the corner of my couch and just waited. I usually had my phone in my hand, glancing back and forth between that and the television. This time, I kinda knew what was coming, so I stared off into space or just at the floor. The last call that was listed in it was an hour ago, when I told a friend to come through at nine. She always arrived five minutes early, no matter where we were going. She had literally just walked in the crib at 8:55. She was putting groceries up, because I told her to come thru so we could do our thing and cook a little something for the next few days. I saw life in a bottle of water, containing that oh so ever precious oxygen we have all come to love on the table. I reached for it. In the midst of that, I fell over onto the floor between the table and the couch. I told myself that I was alright, but I knew it was over. I tried to roll over, but to no avail. I was dead as soon as I hit the floor. In preparation for this, I left my living room sliding window wide open. I knew the summer breeze would carry my soul all the way to the next life. As I had learned from studying the Ancient Egyptians, death was just the beginning and that my real journey was just beginning. Hopefully, Osiris let me pass through. Faintly, I remember hearing baby girl's voice, screaming for me to get up. She always was there for me and not just for the physical. How she stayed, still trying to be after me after I didn't commit, I will forever wonder. I heard her continue to scream, but the life was sucked out of me at that point. By the time she was calling 911, I was dead. You know how the story ends. They put me in an ambulance, neighbors probably outside looking on because they were naturally curious. You know white people made sure to know what was going on at all times. They'll probably bring me back once, but with what I had in my system, I knew it wouldn't last long. I was dead. Gone. I don't know where my spirit would end up, but I do know that mere days before I went, I updated everything in my will. Everything and I mean everything, is left for you. Along with the cash, you'll find the deed to my crib in Portland. It's yours. My cars, they ain't yours. Just a car. I purchased a Bentley in Bellevue, Washington when I went back for that week. It was between that, the 2018 Mercedes S Class and a Maserati. Trust me when I tell you, rich people spend money. Don't believe that they all live like they are poor just because you see a meme of Bill Gates in a polo. Everything is paid off. All you have to do is maintain it. Also, you got 49 suits in the closet. Remember that day I told you to get a polo and some jeans from Ross? Well, that was my plan to get you to start looking like a man. So, when we stopped in the suit store in Fargo that day, and you fought me like a newborn not to get a suit, I managed to still achieve the goal of getting you to see your future. All 49 of these are custom made. You have 22 one-piece joints. You have 27 three-piece joints. Not to mention every color in the alphabet of shirts, belts and lizard skins. Why 49 you ask? Simple. I got buried in suit number 50. Peanut brown shirt, ivory tie and a chocolate checkerboard joint, with a hint of ivory in the stripes. Trust me. I am as fresh underground as I was above ground. Gone is the struggle of Soundview and North Dakota. Now, it's to the big city once again. It's not New York by any means, and black culture in Portland is few and far between. But, you have grown enough to know what's becoming of a man and what is not. When I first started really taking you under my wing, you were stealing top ramen packs and putting them inside of your coat. When I last left you, you were angry with me, but you yelled at me in polos and jeans that were loose, but not baggy. Cleavon and I talked about you on a daily. He was terminally ill, yet he never looked the part and he never told anyone. This whole year and beyond led up to this moment right here. If you recall, I once told you all lies aren't bad. Parents tell children year in and year out that they can become the President of the United States. We know with deep thinking that the president is always selected and never elected. The democracy component is an illusion to make people think that the power rest in their hands. But, telling your child that they can be anything is not bad at all. I told you a lot about me that wasn't true. But, here you are, set for life. Remember, sometimes the biggest lie, can be the most beautiful truth. Don't worry about cleaning off my grave. I got buried and laid down into the Portland soil, at a house out in an area called Southwest Hills. Just follow the huge Oak tree with a blue ribbon on it to find out where. Oh yeah. That old man house I was buried at, his company put up the money for the magazine company, which has turned into a multi-million-dollar empire. One night, he deposited $500,000 in my guys bank account and then glitched his account to take it out all in his name. No loss to him. The bank I cashed it at, his family owns that as well. You've learned a lot over the time I've known you. Just keep the empire going. See you at the crossroads. P.S. Remember. Legends never die.

My lady friends ask me all the time. Antwon. Bruh. What do I have to do to keep these men happy? It seems like I'm always running into losers. "Well girl. Maybe. Just maybe. It's you that needs to change and recognize your own mistakes. I always tell you that, but it seems like you don't wanna hear the shit." Keara did what she always did when she asked for my opinion. She rolled her eyes and walked off. I took a sip of the cranberry juice, seeing how I didn't drink. Well, not yet. It was crazy. What women don't realize though is that keeping a man is quite simple. Here are ten ways to do that, especially in the year of twenty-one nine.

10. Learn to listen to your man.

    By listening, I mean listening to understand what it is he is trying to convey to you. It does not mean listening to respond. A rebuttal isn't always needed.

9. Don't make little issues bigger issues.

    Learn to control your emotions just a little bit more. Little things that can be fixed or ignored shouldn't result in a full-fledged argument.

8. Be his comfort zone not his battle field.

    He should look forward to coming home or to be with you. If he has to fight with you every day, he will become more and more distracted by the 'Happiness' that is being portrayed elsewhere.

7. Allow him to be a Man.

    I don't know how many times I've seen women say "Men don't know how to be men," but somehow you do? Stop it. I'm sure he won't be perfect, but it's the effort in which he puts in. So, what he didn't buy you a diamond necklace for your birthday. The effort he put into taking you out to dinner and catering to your every need should be enough. Yes, I know we all have different love languages or whatever, but everything shouldn't be spoken in your native tongue when in a relationship.

6. Compliment Him.

Contrary to popular belief, Men love being complimented. You are his woman. If you don't tell him how sexy you think he is or how awesome you feel when he is around, he will search elsewhere for the validation. And yes, I don't care how much of a man's man he says he is. We all need validation from a woman no matter if it's our woman or not. Side note: That's what side chicks are good at.

5. Encourage him.

There is nothing worse than a woman that belittles a man. No matter if he is financially unstable or sexually unsatisfactory, belittling him is only pushing him into the arms of somebody that appreciates what he brings to the table and encourages him to do better. A little motivation goes a very long way. You'd be surprised.

4. Be respectable.

I see it all the time. Females in relationships get in these Facebook groups and let their inner whore seep through.

Do y'all not realize how you look? Talking about what your sex game is like to strangers isn't appealing at all. Trust that it will get back to your man eventually. Which brings me to my next point.

3. Be trustworthy.

Men are prideful creatures as you may know, so seeing our woman flirting online or gushing over other men plays on a man's psyche. His mind begins to wander. And, since he can't prove it, he might as well get a backup plan too just in case.

2. Allow him to be the star player on your team.

As a sports fan, I understand the importance of teamwork, but on all of the great teams, someone has to be the star. Now don't get me wrong. You will have your moment in the spotlight. But, allow him to shine bright. It's for the greater good of the team. And if you do have a good man, he won't mind sharing the spotlight a little more.

1. SUCK HIS DICK.

The most important part of reducing the chances of him cheating is oral pleasure. There are still women out there that don't do it. I don't know what to tell you. If you ain't sucking on demand or even spontaneously throughout the week, you are getting cheated on. No questions asked.

BONUS TIP: Have a plan and execute it. Or, if you don't have a plan, help him execute his.

I learned this game from Cleavon and the stories he told me of his escapades back in Chicago. He never settled down with one woman, but he did always keep one of value to him. What do I mean you ask? Cleavon always used to preach to me one thing. "Son. Never fuck with a woman who can't do anything for you." Now, OG wasn't talking about sexual favors or cooking. None of that shit. That was all basic stuff that a woman should do in the first place. What OG was referring to is that if you keep women on your team, you gotta ensure that each one of them has a role that they play. And, that role needs to be vital. Take the 1996 Chicago Bulls for example. That starting lineup was indeed special. Rodman handled the rebounds. Pip was the prime defender. Jordan. Well. Jordan just did what he did. Ron Harper was the hidden spark. They didn't need him to be the 20 and 9 guy he had been up to that point in his career. All they needed for him to do was play an additional scoring role. Space the floor, give 'em eight to ten a game, and they were good. Luc Longley. Well. He just needed to take up space. See, it was the same thing with women. You needed each one on your squad to play a vital role in your everyday life needs. You needed you a numbers woman. She may not have necessarily been an accountant, but she was good with the finances. She knew how to maintain, invest and flip money. She knew when to buy and pull stocks. She knew how to manage the credit game. She knew how to negotiate a price to the point where she could save you 80% on a good, even though you didn't save 80%. You needed you a health woman. This is by far the most underutilized woman as far as men goes. No, she doesn't have to be a vegan. She can simply be an exercise guru. She knows the proper herbs needed to lower the blood pressure, boost your immune system, keep your skin clear, all that. She knew how to relieve stress through yoga. She knew how to make a meal, have it taste good, but it benefited your body in numerous ways. See you couldn't excel in life if you were pumped up on medications and struggling to get around. Actually, when you thought about it, you got a health chick and a chef all in one. Then, the next woman you needed on your team was the gangster chick. Ok, ok. Now, hear me out on this one. I am in no way talking about the one who stays in section 8, wears a scarf and will stomp somebody out for you. Naw, not that gangster chick. I'm talking about the chick who can hit your enemies and naysayers where it hurts. In the pockets. Most of these women are called attorneys and lawyers. They know how to fight a battle without getting physical. If someone is messing with your livelihood, they know how to take the fight back to them tenfold. Not to mention that a woman in a dress and heels, who spent all day on a case only wanted to be knocked down thoroughly when the day was done. Another chick that you needed to keep on your team was the plug. She is the plug for everything. Need some tickets for an event, holla at her. Cheap airline passes, holla at her. The plug is probably one of the most important pieces that everyone has, but they aren't of the same caliber. Some plugs are only good for clubs. Nah. You don't want that type of plug. You need the plug that can benefit you to where whatever she plugs you with, it will benefit your soul as an individual. I took heed to my OG's words, as I thought about the few times that I stood over his gravesite back in North Dakota. It had been almost a year since my life had changed and it seemed like I ended up here by accident. People have this notion of saying that people die prematurely, but I didn't believe so. I truly believed that everyone died when their purpose on earth was over. It's just sometimes, that purpose is for another person to learn a lesson. There were many lessons that I learned in my short years of life that hadn't even hit 21 yet. The buildup, however, to all of it, was the shit that made me the man that I was today.

"Yo, like why you ain't never doing nothing dawg? You be cooped up with ya computer all damn day bruh? You don't even come and hang out on weekends anymore. I know you ain't scared of the big-time man, cause you living it. Your ass used to jump off this porch every damn rip. Man, bartender, let me get that drank mane? Crown straight. Two shots." The bartender got his drink and passed the additional shot to RU. He turned that damn glass upside down like he was a fish inhaling a group of plankton. "So, fam bam. What's this shit you be doing? Muthafucka paid like shit." I looked at Ru and laughed, as I took another sip of my cranberry juice. "E Commerce."

"The fuck is that?," Skunk asked me. I turned back around to look at him. This was like the scene from Boyz N the Hood where they were all chilling on the porch of Doughboy's house, chopping it up. I knew he would never understand it, but how could you blame him? When he woke up in the morning, he saw heroin addicts. When I woke up in the morning, I saw trees and white picket fences. "I mean. It's basically selling shit online." RU looked at me with a smirk. "Man, what the fuck you know about selling some shit?," as he pushed my head. "I'm online and it's about meeting a bitch." Skunk let out a laugh behind him and dapped him up. "You feel me blood. That's where you meet the hoes at. Or set some fools up. Man, you got me trying to be preppy blood. Matter fact, here. Take a swig of this. That suburbia shit got you all assed out in the head." Fam handed me the Crown Royal that he hadn't even downed yet and ordered another one. I took a hard swig, even though I wasn't supposed too. "Damn man don't drool all over my shit. Give a muthafucka aids or something."

"Man please."

"Oh shit. Who is this nigga?," Skunk said. RU grabbed a napkin and wiped his mouth, as we all were now looking at this cat from the outside bar. Homeboy got out of his red beamer. He got out cleaner than a pork rib in a fat man's mouth. He began to walk up. I then recognized who he was.

"How y'all brothers doing? Twon my dude."

"Imhotep what's poppin' my dude," as I stuck my hand out and we shook. "This Ron and Scotty." I could tell RU wasn't used to this young business shit because he was lowkey preparing for a battle. Skunk wasn't either. Wasn't no way that I was gonna introduce those two niggas by their street names. Not when my business partner was around. I was trying to get these ignat niggas to see another side of life. One

174

that involves real freedom and not looking over your shoulder all the damn time. "Yo lite bright nigga. I'm RU, as in Piru nigga." Tep looked dead at me. "You drunk off some of that shit bro?"

"What's brackin then nigga?," as Ru got up from his stool, Skunk right beside em. "Whoa, whoa y'all. Chill," as I now was in between them all. "Calm down. Ru, he ain't on no banging shit bruh. Just cause a nigga in a blue button up don't mean he banging. This my mans. Chill. You too Skunk." Tep was just standing there as if he was waiting for something to pop off, not flinching at all. "Now, let's all sit down and enjoy a drink. Damn sure don't need these white folks calling the cops." Cooler heads prevailed as Ru and Skunk took their seats reluctantly. Tep just shook it off, with a smirk that spoke volumes coming across his face. "So, what you drinking man?," I asked Tep. "Looking like a thousand bucks."

"Well this thousand ass brother need some Yak."

"**YAK!!!** Boy what you know about some damn Yak?" I was waiting for the gotcha to come and really have him go in on me. "Man, I'm serious."

"And nigga I'm serious too. What you know about some muthafuckin Yak? That's an old man drink?"

"I know you don't know shit about it either seeing how yo ass still a baby."

"Midnight my nigga." Tep looked at his watch. "Yeah, well you still got a few hours left. Lemme sit down man."

"Yo we'll holla at you later blood. See you got business going and shit," Skunk said, as him and Ru got up, giving me and Tep some fucked up looks. "You know," Tep said. "If you

175

gone pick some niggas to hang around. Make sure they ain't some crazy niggas." All I could do was laugh. "Now I know you think it's funny cause them Omarr's nutty ass cousins from Southeast, but man. Fuck that." Tep ordered up his drank and pulled out a black. "Damn fool. You smoke black and mild's too?" Tep looked back at me. **"MILDS WITH THAT YAK!!!"**

"Ok Uncle Shannon."

"SKIP!!!" My dude was on some other shit I swear. As we continued on with the night, counting down til my 21st, Tep started telling me about a date he had with a young thang from Seattle. At the end of the night, she ended up getting cut loose. I mean, some women didn't understand. The date was to treat 'em, yes. However, there was a part they had to play in the whole dating experience as well. So, with that, ladies, here is your ten rules for a first date. Y'all ain't off the hook. And I can say this shit better than Cleavon ever could, 'cause I was still a young gunna. Pay attention to rule #9.

---

1. Be ready on time. A man is spending time on the road, money on gas and has prepared himself in his best clothes. The last thing he needs is to arrive at your house and you still ain't ready to leave. If you're dealing with a military man, he will just pull off and go back home. 15 minutes early, you on time. On time, you are late. Please, realize that our time is valuable.

2. Be direct. Don't play any games. If there is something you need or if there is a request, ask us. We aren't mind readers, and if you don't say some things, you won't receive them.

3. Don't ask dumb questions. If this man takes you to Olive Garden, then it's obvious that he is on an Olive Garden budget. Don't ask do you mind if I order this? If he took you there, then obviously 99.9% of the items on the menu are in his price range. Just order.

4. Be courteous. This bounces off #3. Don't go to a restaurant and order the most expensive s**t just to see what he gone say or just because, and know you ain't gonna eat it. That's disrespectful and you have just put yourself in the NCAA tournament category. You will be a one and done date.

5. If you go to the bathroom, go to the bathroom. Do not use your bathroom breaks to text your homegirls about the date. If she is that important, then maybe y'all two need to start dating. You are there for him. Don't be disrespectful.

6. Take care of your priorities beforehand. Do not have that man pull up and you say you can't go because your baby daddy didn't pick the kids up, or something came up that you could've told us hours prior. That's why you call him. Gas is $3.00 a gallon in a lot of places. Now, he has wasted time and money. Had you called prior and informed him, he could've rescheduled, or called female

B, C or D to make new plans. Also, do not expect that man to purchase any food for your kids. Ensure they are fed before you leave the house.

7. We don't wanna hear anything about your past men. We are there to get to know you. If you start talking about your past men, then we will know that you were the problem and you will once again become an NCAA tournament classification. One and done.

8. Leave your problems at home. Don't bring attitudes into your date. You will either be a one and done, that man will turn around and drop you right back off, or he might just leave you at the first destination. Please don't think men aren't petty. Some will leave you downtown to find your way home because of your funky attitude.

9. IMPORTANT. Know some sports. You may not be on a date with anything regarding sports. However, men relate to sports more than anything. If you know he a Georgia Bulldogs football fan, at some random time, hit him with a "So you see that ass whoopin' your boys put on (insert team)?" You just earned some major points in the book.

10. Treat that man how you want to be treated. The date isn't for him to win you over. The date is for y'all to mutually get to know each other better.

Now in the same breath, I have 10 tips for my men also. The young fellas especially need to take notes.

1. Don't ever pull up at a woman's house and text 'Outside'. Pick her up at the door. If you are too lazy to walk up to her door, or if you have to debate your life before walking up to the door (I.E. she stays in the hood and its 30 negros outside her apartment building), you shouldn't be messing with her.

2. You don't need the expensive restaurant. The first date is to get to know each other and the expensive restaurant don't guarantee that you will get the draws. Do something different. Go indoor rock climbing, ride the beach while eating tacos and sing some mutual songs in the car. Clown around with her. Have fun.

3. Don't overdo the compliments. Upon picking her up, let her know she look good, nice, beautiful, whatever you wanna call it. Don't be repeating that shit all night. She'll think you're trying too hard, because you are.

4. **. MAKE SURE YOUR WHIP IS CLEAN AND YOUR CLOTHES ARE PRESSED!!!** If you live in California, there are too many Mexican car washes that will clean and vacuum your whip for $8. You have no excuse for a dirty car.

5. Plan the date. Tell her what type of clothes to be wearing prior. Don't pick her up for a date at the paintball course, and she has come out in the fuck 'em dress (we will discuss this later). It's your job to inform her.

6. Don't ever imply Netflix and chill for a first date. You might as well be prepped for an L.

7. The fuck 'em dress. Every woman has the fuck 'em dress. Meaning it's the dress where she wants your eyes to bulge and she probably got some plans on fucking you afterwards. If she is in the fuck 'em dress, be on your best behavior. Open doors, pull out chairs, don't stare. Be relaxed and act like you've been there before, cause we've all had some ass before. You are more than likely going on a classy date. At the end of the night, **YOU LET HER** invite you in. Don't ask can you come in. Now, if the date has went well and she let you in, congrats. Have fun. She planned on giving you some hours before she left the house. Proceed to blow her back out.

8. Study your female subject. More than likely, y'all have conversed before the date, getting to know the basics of each other. Preparation is key. If she likes fitness and you like fitness, you might consider hitting the gym for a first date and getting protein shakes afterwards. Don't pick a woman up and head for the opera, and neither one of y'all like it.

9. Stay off your phone. She needs your attention. You want her attention. Inform her of possible emergency calls (I.E. kids if you have 'em, or business). That's the quickest way for her to lose interest. You got her to talk too. Call your boys afterwards.

10. Be drama free on your date. Whatever happened with your ex, at work, with your kids, leave that shit at home. She doesn't need to hear that.

As we continued to rap throughout the night, the time hit a quarter til twelve. "What's your aspirations for your grown man status man?," Tep said that a little bit slurred, as he had one too many. "You know man," as I blew an authentic Cuban. "Triple my net worth and my network." Tep grabbed a glass of Yak and held it in the air. "My nigga." I ain't have shit but a glass of melted ice but fuck it. We toasted to that. I drunk mine, but he held back on his. "Man, we just did a toast. You done?"

"Yeah man. Gotta start drinking water. I may have bread, but I ain't trying to lose it over anything stupid."

"Man, I'll take you home."

"Man please. I got a $100,000 car in valet right now. I ain't leaving my shit. Speaking of shit." I whipped my head around as two other brothers in suits headed over. "Damn man. You fucked up Tep?"

"Like yo jump shot." Tep smacked me on my chest. "Yo Twon. These my guys. Terrelle and Lamar. Big time entrepreneurs. Figured you know I'd bring in ya birthday with more connections and shit."

"What y'all brothers do for a living?"

"I write," said Terrelle. "I get bread in all different directions dawg. Daygo style."

"I could definitely fuck with that my nigga." I dapped both these brothers up and they joined us. By the time midnight hit, we all had glasses of champagne, and toasted to the good life. I was officially a legal grown man as America saw it, so I doubled up and ordered two full glasses of that Henn Dog. Grown folks' music blared through the speakers as we all got to know each other more in depth. By one o'clock, it was time to call it a night. Tep had drunk at least 12 glasses of water and seemed sober as all to be damn. I got the numbers of the other two brothers as they were good and buzzed, and said my goodbyes to everyone. I headed over to valet parking so they could bring me my baby. The Bentley rolled smooth as ever. I was finally 21 and the shit felt good. It took me about 40 minutes to get to the crib in Tualatin, but it was a fun ass ride. I didn't have any plans for the rest of the week. I parked the car at exactly 2:02 a.m. I was gonna throw these clothes off as soon as I hit the inside and plop my tired ass right in my bed. I hovered my digital key in front of the lock and opened my door. I was frozen stiff at the sight that was in my house. Here, a young lady was on my couch, in a shiny tangerine robe. The negro in me told me to go ham sandwich. But, this shit was a little too calm. "And who are you may I ask?," as I shut the door behind me. She raised up off the couch. She had silky long hair. And, I couldn't see it yet, but I could tell she had a banging ass body underneath that robe. "I'm Seshat."

"Oh. Like the Egyptian goddess."

"Yeah."

"Well," as if I really had any questions because I know what was about to happen. "How did you get in here?" That's when she pulled out a digitized key out of a pocket in her robe. She held it up in her right hand. "It's what he left me in the will. He groomed me out of North Portland since I was a teen. And I'm 21 tonight. So, I figure since we now grown, that we grow this empire together. Oh yeah, by the way, I got this package on the table for you." I looked over, and it was a manila envelope. After she said that, she dropped her robe. "Happy birthday," she said. Yeah oh yeah. Indeed, it was for damn sure about to be one banging ass birthday. All pun intended. I woke up about a quarter past noon. Baby girl was still out. I didn't even remember her name at this point. All I know was that the cooch was soaking and her head was flame. I got up to go take a pis and feed the fishes of the Pacific Ocean. As I washed my hands, I thought about the package that was left on the living room table. I scooted my tired, yet happy tail in the living room in my draws and grabbed it. I looked at it. Five words were written on it. The Square Root of Truth. I opened it up. In it, was a CD with the words "play me" written on it. Man, if this wasn't some crazy ass Saw shit. I walked back towards the bedroom. Baby girl was still sprawled out on the bed. I laughed softly. I put that empire in her New York style, cause that's what I do. I walked over to grab my laptop and my headphones. Baby girl was still a mystery, so whatever was on the disk may not have been for her ears. I placed the laptop on the couch and put the disk in, connecting my headphones. It seemed like when you wanted to see some shit, the computer took forever to cut on. Finally, after what seemed like forever, my home screen showed up. I clicked on the disk option and hit play when made available. I watched it buffer for like eight seconds until an ocean popped up with the waves crashing everywhere. Wherever this was, it was lovely. Then, the camera started to rotate around. I paused it and dropped my headphones, getting up from the couch and walking around. It was Darnell. I caught my breath after about a full two minutes and sat back down on the couch. I put my headphones on and un paused the video. "What's up Antwon? Yo, I can't call you Twon anymore cause you a grown ass man. I know, I know. This was the last thing that you were expecting to see. Well, first off, happy birthday my man. I know you living it up, especially with that booty that you tore up last night. Yeah man. I been knowing Seshat since she was a kid man. Her mama, she was the one at the house calling 911 when, you know, I died. Anyways, let me tell you what really happened." Just then, I saw a bomb ass woman come into the picture and bring him a drink. "Thank you love," Darnell said, planting a kiss on her lips. "Oh man. This Seshat moms. We clicking for life right now. Any who. My man's use to tell me to follow the trail of the wealthy white man and you can never go wrong. Well, that's what I did. So peep right. What I drunk that night, I still have no clue. However, I had my man's Johnny Black look up some shit that would pretty much put me out for 24 hours. Now, on some real shit. You are out in a matter of five minutes. I don't remember anything to be honest with you. When I woke up, I was in a room, surrounded by some highly important people. You ain't think I was gonna actually kill myself did you. Any who, I won't be seen again. Ever. Not in the states. Neither will ol' girl's mom. We been rocking since we were kids, and I always told her when I'm right, she gone be right for life. So, I'm not telling you where I'm at. Just know, ya boy good. I got enough money over here to last me forty lifetimes. As for you, let me let you in on some more shit. Seshat, she was in the will to. Her key was left. Y'all born on the same day. Y'all both been groomed by the best. An empire is yours. Fuck, travel, fuck some more and love each other. That's what y'all do. Oh, by the way, if you look in the section of the fridge where the butter is kept, you'll see a little something else that was left for you. Think of it in a metaphoric stance. But, on some real shit, all your connects, you know 'em. Keep fucking with Tep, and the money trail gone keep growing. And always, always remember. Follow the trail of the wealthy white man, and you will never go wrong. Peace out family." The video screen then went black. Shocked was severely an understatement. I took off the headphones, as all I could do at this point was laugh. I shook it off and walked over to the refrigerator. I looked were the butter was. There were four sticks to be exact. I knew damn well he ain't want me to find the Imperial, so I emptied it out. Beneath all those sticks, I found a quarter and a sticky note. "Read the book of Luke," it said. I didn't get it, but in time, I was sure that I would. I just smiled. My guy was right. The biggest lies can sometimes lead to the best truths. "Antwon?" I turned around to see Seshat in her robe, peeking around the wall. "What's going on love?" From behind the wall, she held out her robe and dropped it on the floor. "I'm hungry. Come in the room and feed me breakfast." She smiled and disappeared. Man, fuck this quarter and note right now. I'll find out the meaning of that later. Right now, I had to go handle business. The wealthy white man may have led to the money trail, but the fine back woman was leading me to the love trail.

I'll holla at y'all.

ABOUT THE AUTHOR

IT IS EASY for a man to perform in front of a crowd when everyone is cheering for him. However, the true test of a man is how he performs on the biggest stage amidst the boos from the crowd. No one ever built strength in a peaceful environment. These are the words of renown author Joe R. McClain Jr. To his credit, Mr. Joe McClain Jr. has penned eight novels, with two becoming best sellers on Amazon. His book BANDAGES, reached #1. His fourth novel, A Black Man Has 9 Lives, peaked at #29. What started in 2013 as a hobby has turned into a journey that he couldn't even see himself going on. His writings have sold all over the world in Pakistan, Afghanistan, Japan, The UK, Australia, Malaysia and over 11 countries in all. They have even been obtained by some of the most prolific people in the entertainment industry to include members of Floyd Mayweather's Money Team, Mark Cuban, Wu Tang Clan co-founder GZA, actor Duane Martin, Grammy Award winning R&B singer/songwriter Eric Bellinger, NBA Hall of Famer Kareem Abdul-Jabbar and many more. His publishing company, Uprock Publications, which is ran by his business partner and Chief Executive Officer Caujuan Mayo, has penned several top 30 bestselling novels since 2012. This success has led to many marketing and brand opportunities, which has included expansion in support of many active NFL players and alumni. With a reading and writing initiative that attempts to increase literacy and writing comprehension in urban environments throughout America, his purpose is one that will benefit youth and young adults for many years to come. Only content.

Coming Soon

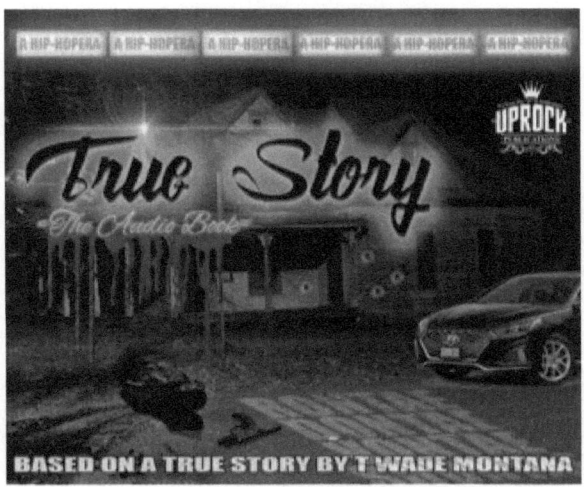

The first Hip-Hopera Audio Book Based on a True Story told in a unique way through rap. The story of a scandalous female caught up in love triangle that ultimately cost a life and sends two others to prison.

Now Available For Purchase

Plantation Chains

Two friends. Two brothers. Two men that would go to the ends of the world and back for each other. That's the type of relationship that Wayne "Ty" Russell and Kevin West had. However, the two men had different plans for their lives. One loved the bright lights of the big city. The other wanted to grind it out aggressively, leaving his mark in some of the most random places on Earth. Upon going their separate ways, they will learn the definite meaning of friendship and what it means to truly be loyal to a cause.

The Writer's Block

A Short Story

When his father passed at 12, Mr. Terrelle Washington grew up fast and survived the dangerous streets of East Chicago, Indiana. After finding out his deceased father left him a large inheritance, he decided to leave for California and achieve his dream of becoming a published author. However, the land of Hollywood stars was soon transformed into a maze of unforeseen obstacles he never expected on his way to the top. How will it play out??? Will he achieve his dream, or will it be shattered into a nightmare of failure?

P.E.E.R.S

The Five Step Process Towards Achieving Greatness

Joe McClain Jr. has taken the book world by storm over the past few years. Now, as he grows to a high level in his craft, he presents to his readers P.E.E.R.S: The five-step process towards achieving greatness. Joe has taken his love for motivating the masses and put it all in this easy to follow the guide of steps you can take to achieve greatness here on earth. The author/poet/motivational speaker opens up on all aspects of his life and everyone's in general, giving you the tools you need to build empires. No, this book will not tell you how to get rich overnight or become the next great singer. It can, however, start you off in the right direction to begin the process of elevating yourself to levels you could have never imagined. P.E.E.R.S. is a powerful book that many of this generation will be talking about for years to come.

Sleeping with the Lights On

Lamar Atteley III has made out a good life for himself. He has turned Las Vegas into his own personal playground after surviving the rough environment of Detroit, Michigan. However, with a new job offer, he now has to prepare for a new chapter of his life that will either make or break him. His adventure will take him to the other side of the  world......to Guam. Now, he will be tested harder than any other point in his life. With all new surroundings, more money, women at his disposal and a different breed of people in general, the question is can he handle it all. When its all said and done, you will understand why we sometimes sleep with the lights on.

Bandages

A hard life in the inner city. Made it through. About to prepare for the next step of most young men. College. That was all until one fateful night to where freedom was taken away. Now, in the battle of his young life, a young man has two options. Die in prison, or snitch and possibly get another chance. Either choice will draw consequences, but what will he choose??? What wounds will be healed, and what wounds will be re-opened???

A Black Man Has 9 Lives

Ramses Osiris Martin wasn't like the typical black kid growing up in America. He had it made in life. He lived in a good neighborhood in Southern California, with wealthy parents and went to the best schools money could buy. However, even with all of that, he still faced a challenge that no doctor or amount of money could cure. That was simply

trying to face the reality of what it is really like to be Black in America. Separated from his culture due to where he grew up, the young 16-year-old is now on a journey to see who he really is. A simple trip to unfamiliar lands will test him to the very depths of his soul. Throughout it all, it will take him through hell and back. From the football field to the country, the inner city and beyond, what lessons will stay entrenched in his soul for all eternity? What is the price that he will pay to see how deep the melanin roots are in his skin?

Bandages 2

Star Jackson is pregnant and seeing her husband off for a six month deployment to The Persian Gulf. With Carl gone, Star will take herself out of her comfort zone and go search for the answers to her past which she so desperately seeks. However, during her journey, she will get many answers that she was not prepared for. In turn, it will open up many memories that lay dormant that are now seeking to devour her. With her husband gone and no one to lean on but herself, she must overcome the opening of old wounds and heal new ones. In a race to find the truth, she will learn that the biggest threat to healing is facing yourself.

Broken Locks

Welcome to Goodman Park, U.S.A. Population slightly under 3,000. It's a small, Midwest town nestled in the heart of industrial America, with the majority of its residents being black. Here, everyone knows everyone and the community take care of each other. Tre Matthews is one of those residents. A well known young man whose athletic talents took him to the University of Georgia. However, upon his return home after college, the town is discovered to be sitting on poisoned land. The whole community is threatened with being pushed out. Upon learning of this, he tries to rally support from whoever will listen to save his community. In his travels, he meets someone who will end up being the Key to unlocking a chain reaction that may save his town, or destroy it all together in the end.

Let Me Pimp Or Let Me Die
Till Game Do Us Part

Ricky Walters grew up in the gritty streets of San Diego California. Upon quitting his security job, he meets an ex-pimp name Trust who teaches him everything about the pimp game. Ricky ends up turning out a young Asian girl name Yuki, changes his name to Jackpot, and jumps knee deep in the pimp game. Jackpot makes a conscious decision to become the biggest pimp to ever play the game and goes cross country. Here, is where Jackpot finds himself getting money, ducking the police, feuding with haters, vindictive females, snitches, and eventually doing time in the penitentiary.

Let Me Pimp Or Let Me Die 2
The Hoe Chronicles

Let Me Pimp Or Let Me Die 2, tells the story of a few female workers in the "Game," told through their lives as you see and find out what motivates a woman to start ho'n and sell her body. Re-visit some of your favorite characters from part 1 and see what drove them into the lifestyle that they chose. Each story different but ultimately the same.

Graphic and not for the faint of heart, the scenes take place in a realistic setting with many twist n turns you won't see coming. Find out how F.A.B Killed Sunshine and what happened in those last moments. How Green Eyes got hooked on drugs and the real reason she left Jackpot for dead in prison. Or the number one question… Will Jackpot Return To The Game?

Fresh Out

Jamal Hicks, also known as J-Bone, a Young O.G. from the notorious Skyline East Side Piru Bloods, is fresh out and on a mission to do right. Life on the streets as an ex-con proves to be hard as the struggle forces J-Bone back to his old ways. Now the set is divided, homies are at war, his best friend Dee slept with his girlfriend while locked up and are now sworn, enemies. Death, murder, mayhem, kidnap and robbery will all take place and plague JBone's world. All the while...still being, FRESH OUT!

Cooking With Weed

Wake n Bake the natural way. Weed consumption through digestion is a lot healthier than smoking it, which is why we put together this book of tasty meals with a 420 kick to keep you happy, smiling and feeling good! From breakfast, lunch, dinner to dessert we got you covered. Enjoy some

weed laced french toast for breakfast. Craving a light snack? Try some of our weed hummus. End the night with a homemade weed pizza and cheesecake for dessert. We even have a recipe for cooking oil and weed butter. Over 30 different recipes to choose from. Meals so quick and easy to make, you'll wonder why you didn't pick up this book sooner. Simple everyday recipes made easy will have you feeling like a pro in the kitchen! No more having to buy overpriced edibles from the dispensary. Now you can make all those delicious treats yourself.

Xavier Sands and Danielle Seville meet at the grand opening of Xavier's nightclub, and it happens to be his birthday. Not to be left out, Danielle is celebrating her birthday as well. As the two grow closer, wedges are driven between them behind the scenes, by their own mothers!

Xavier and Danielle both work for King Kole Konners, in different venues, but when the King is shot, all bets are off. The kingdom having just survived the Chase St. John mutiny in South Nubia, is rocked once again. The assassin begins picking off the King's top people, leading to Danielle being kidnapped.

Xavier vows vengeance on the person, or persons responsible for the shooting of the King. During her kidnapping ordeal, Danielle learns a horrible, life-changing secret. Just as her world is rocked, Xavier learns the same shocking truth from his mother.

The assassin and the criminal masquerading as a cop, joins forces with Xavier and Danielle, as they set out to dethrone the great King Kole Konners! The Family Honor has been breached from within. The only question is, can the Seed ascend to the throne?